NICO

The Mavericks, Book 08

Dale Mayer

NICO: THE MAVERICKS, BOOK 8
Beverly Dale Mayer
Valley Publishing Ltd.

ISBN-13: 978-1-773362-94-6
Print Edition

About This Book

What happens when the very men—trained to make the hard decisions—come up against the rules and regulations that hold them back from doing what needs to be done? They either stay and work within the constraints given to them or they walk away. Only now, for a select few, they have another option:

The Mavericks. A covert black ops team that steps up and break all the rules … but gets the job done.

Welcome to a new military romance series by *USA Today* best-selling author Dale Mayer. A series where you meet new friends and just might get to meet old ones too in this raw and compelling look at the men who keep us safe every day from the darkness where they operate—and live—in the shadows … until someone special helps them step into the light.

With barely enough time to recover from helping out Miles in London, Nico is off to Australia … and a secret mission involving a US covert operative …

When an American undercover operative's sister goes missing in Australia, Nico has to find out if this is connected to the operative or to the sister's own activist background. Apparently she made enemies easily.

Charlotte hadn't wanted to make this trip in the first place, preferring to communicate her polarizing messages through writing her books now. But, bowing under pressure, she finally arrives in Australia, only to be attacked within minutes of reaching her hotel room for the night. After her rescue, she's forced to dig deep into her family and public life to find the mastermind kidnapper and to stay safe as the bodies pile up.

Nothing makes sense in this twisted mission, but Nico is determined to keep Charlotte safe, even as things take a more personal turn …

Sign up to be notified of all Dale's releases here!
https://geni.us/DaleNews

Books in This Series

Kerrick, Book 1

Griffin, Book 2

Jax, Book 3

Beau, Book 4

Asher, Book 5

Ryker, Book 6

Miles, Book 7

Nico, Book 8

Keane, Book 9

Lennox, Book 10

Gavin, Book 11

Shane, Book 12

Diesel, Book 13

Jerricho, Book 14

Killian, Book 15

Hatch, Book 16

Corbin, Book 17

Aiden, Book 18

Boxed Sets and Bundles
https://geni.us/Bundlepage

CHAPTER 1

NICO STRATUS STARED at his phone in disbelief. A message from Miles. Nico had been expecting it but, at the same time, hadn't *really* been expecting it. Like one of those things that he knew was coming, yet he just didn't know when. But days ago he'd expected it, and, when it didn't come, he'd relaxed. The timing was really crappy right now. He had groceries in his shopping cart in front of him, and he was just halfway through the list in his hand. But then he hadn't been planning on buying very much. Still it was too much. The message from Miles was clear.

Leave now.

Swearing softly, Nico walked away from his shopping cart, knowing that's the last thing he would normally do. He shrugged, not having much choice. When he got outside to his car, he found a 9x13 envelope in the front seat. He snatched it up, read the cover note atop a folder, informing him that he was flying to Australia to a military air base. Also enclosed was one burner phone. He swore.

The flight would be fifteen-and-a-half-hours long. Then the time zone change would add on another seventeen hours. When he landed, the clock would show thirty-two and a half hours later. For him. But, for their kidnap victim, it would be closer to twenty hours later by the time he landed in Sydney. Never a good thing in a kidnapping matter to not find the victim in the first twenty-four hours. Still she could be long gone. Dead already. Shipped out to another country. Sold into sex slavery. He shook his head. *The travel-related delays can't be helped when we work all over the world.*

He drove home quickly, parked his vehicle in the underground parking, then headed to his apartment and snagged his go-bag. He checked to make sure everything had been replenished though, before he turned and walked out. He had no idea when he'd be back. He was currently living in San Diego, close to the Coronado military base. That meant a fast military flight out. He was grateful for that. Like having his own private jet at his disposal.

As he hopped into the cab awaiting him—thanks to Miles and the Mavericks—and was driven to the airport, Nico studied the files in the folder. His itinerary was there, as well as a dossier. He stared at it and shook his head, whispering, "Seriously, an American activist is in trouble? Isn't that understood in that line of work? Why the hell am I involved in something like this?"

Just then his new burner phone beeped, and a series of texts rolled through. But they were all from Ryker.

Parcel waiting for you at the airport. More burner phones. All communication must be dark.

He quickly texted back. **Does anybody know I'll be there?**

Only your partner.

And the Australian government is okay with this?

Not likely but they don't know. And we're not telling them at this time. If we can keep this op a secret, we need to.

Seriously?

Yes. There are added layers to this issue that we can't put down on paper. We need this to be a totally

blacked-out version of black ops. You'll get all the help you need regardless.

And why aren't the Australian police handling this on their own?

We prefer to keep this in-house.

Can't we use them without telling them about the layers?

We may. Later. But, for now, we are relying on you.

And what happened? Start from the beginning.

A prominent activist has gone missing.

Great. No lack of suspects then. He shook his head. **When and where?**

She was over there for a big rally in support of the indigenous people and their problems, plus the injustices to all humanity in the face of the climate issues. She was supposed to give a big speech. Only she never showed.

She just disappeared?

From her hotel room, yes.

And she's been reported as a missing person?

Yes. The local police are aware of this, but our government has asked theirs to let us be the primary investigators.

He waited because, of course, if the local cops were looking into this, even in a secondary capacity, why was he called in? **And?** he finally texted in exasperation when there was no answer. He looked around outside the cab's windows to see that they were maybe ten minutes away from the airport.

His phone beeped again, and the text read, **She's the sister of somebody high up in our government who is undercover at the moment.**

"So then I'm sure the Australian government and their police authorities will be happy to cooperate," he muttered to himself.

But the answer came back. **And it's top secret.**

Shit. So I can't ask for help?

Not from the regular channels. The American government has already expressed their concerns with the Australian government, and everybody is open and cooperating … but …

But this undercover element is specialized?

Very. They have their own black-op operatives working that end. You will be working the kidnapping end.

Ransom demand?

Not yet. We have very little information on our own.

Do we have any clue as to where she's being kept and why her?

Hope to have a better idea about where she's at when you land. Possibly taken because of her highly public outburst against the treatment of the indigenous people in Australia.

Oh, yeah. That could do it.

Possibly, but then she's been fairly outspoken for a long time, Ryker texted. **She's an anthropologist working around the world to promote better treatment for the original people of every country. And she just happens to be in Australia now.**

Is she the activist author who's been in the news a lot? Nico asked.

Yes, that's her. What we're really concerned about is that our undercover man's been compromised and that she's been taken to control him.

"Shit," Nico said as he picked up his bag and the file and exited the cab, and the driver drove away without even allowing him to pay. He headed to the counter. There, he quickly checked in and ended up in the boarding area, where he had only five minutes before moving onto the flight itself. He had just enough time to pick up the package awaiting him and to stuff it into his carry-on bag. He pulled out his first burner phone and called Ryker again. "I need more information on her and on him," he said.

"You can have more information on her," Ryker said, "but you already know what it's like trying to get any information on him. It's top secret."

"Top secret, my ass. His sister's been taken. Is nobody even considering that maybe it's not so top secret anymore? That the bad guys know more than I do about it right now?"

"That's exactly what they're considering," Ryker said. "But they're not letting out any more information just because of that. She's also caused quite a stir herself with her books anyway."

"She's young, isn't she?"

"She's thirty-three," Ryker said. "Old enough to have caused a lot of people to rethink their treatment of the needs of the people in their lands."

"Or to say that they're rethinking it," Nico said drily.

"Exactly."

"When did she last check into her room via her key card usage?"

"Eleven-thirty last night."

"And when did anybody find out she wasn't there?"

"Eight o'clock this morning, her time. One of her coworkers knocked on the door to meet up for breakfast and to go to the rally."

"And her key wasn't used in the meantime or any master key?"

"Apparently not."

"You and I both know how easy it is to make it appear

that way, when it wasn't."

"It's possible, but we don't know anything yet for sure, which is why you're on your way over there."

"By the time I arrive …"

"You're on the fastest flight. We'll get you there," Ryker said.

"As our Mavericks team grows, we need a man in each of the main continents."

"Working on it."

"We've already got Kerrick in France, Beau in NYC on the opposite coast, Asher in Geneva, Miles in London. I presume the rest of the guys and their women are open to moving as long as they are together."

Ryker laughed. "That's what I understand too. Miles will be your Mavericks contact once you land in Sydney." And, at that, Ryker hung up. The military plane took off not long afterward. With his laptop, Nico did as much research as he could on the long flight, finding out more about the missing woman.

What really interested him was all the online information which said she was an only child.

Yet according to the information he'd gotten from Ryker, this top secret man working undercover was her brother. So, somehow that information had been erased from the records. It always amazed Nico how people thought that would work because, once it was fact, it was somewhere. Still there. Even now.

He just had to find it. He kept digging down, going as far back as into her elementary school years. And there, he found a sibling. But it wasn't at the regular elementary school. She'd gone to another one for just a few months. A casual mention of her and her brother noted them as new members of a chess club, and Nico sat here and stared at that. Wasn't Kerrick's partner, Amanda, the cancer researcher, also a chess player? Something to do with being ultrasmart?

He shook his head, not sure if this had anything to do with that. Our missing activist, Charlotte, had been in grade four at that time, for God's sake. What could genius kids in grade four even do? Apparently they played chess.

Nico kept working his way through the rest of the information available online. She'd been married for five years to Rowe Browning from Arizona. He had been a long-time supporter of Native American rights, and she was halfway through her degree to become an anthropologist. After this marriage, she'd become an ardent protester of the treatment of all the Native people, then her husband had died, six years ago now, and she'd continued the cause afterward and had reverted to her maiden name of Ankerby.

He kept reading, looking at the Australian rally she was to attend and how well advertised it was, only to find her announcement as a keynote speaker at this big event was splashed all over the website. So thousands, if not millions, knew that she was coming here.

Nico was also registered at the same hotel where she had disappeared. That gave him the best access to look for her. She did not travel with security, according to the notes that he had, so, up until now, her own safety hadn't been an issue. He was pretty damn sure that, after this though, that would change. On the other hand, maybe it would calm her down, and she wouldn't be quite so visible. Nothing like the threat of losing your own life—or that of one of your family—in this level of danger for you to rethink your life's plans.

Yet, if this kidnapping was connected to her brother and his secret undercover world, then a whole lot of government rethinking needed to be done here, in Nico's opinion. Not only had the brother been compromised but he had put his sister in danger too. However, if this was connected to the sister's activism, then she could have added another level of danger to her brother's undercover activities. Like her brother needed more reasons why somebody would go after him. If he was black ops and undercover, it meant he was working deep and dealing with other governments.

Somebody somewhere would want him dead no matter who, how, or why. That was just a given, and learning anything more about that wouldn't necessarily help with finding his sister. The information was sketchy on the rest of her life, like who exactly was her husband. A name was here but nothing about what he was like. Why and how did he die? There were again no details.

Nico hated to question his death and life like that but hated even more not having answers. Where had they lived in the US? Just because the husband's family was from Arizona didn't mean they had resided there once they married. That was also where she had gone to school though. He kept digging and finding different layers upon layers and taking his time.

When he finally ran out of questions, most still unanswered, he closed his eyes and tried his hardest to get some sleep. Because, once he landed, he would be filled with an adrenaline rush. Go, go, go. And that just reminded him of something else. He quickly sent a message on one of the six burner phones he'd brought with him.

Am I alone?

No. He'll meet you at the airport.

Nico smiled at that. He had no clue who he was supposedly working with from here on in. He wanted to ask the Mavericks chat window for more details but realized the plane would be landing soon anyway. Nico set his watch to match the current Sydney time zone. It was now Friday, early evening. Regardless, it still felt like the wee morning hours of Coronado to Nico.

By the time Nico got off the flight, he headed straight for the exit and outside. He hadn't been there ten seconds, looking around to see if he recognized anybody, when a vehicle drove up. It was a sports car, something that he'd have picked up himself. He took one look at Keane in the driver's seat and hopped inside. "Well, thank God, it's you." Nico immediately handed him one of the burner phones.

Keane nodded, pocketed the phone, grinned at him, and smacked him hard on the shoulder. "This way you don't get to hug me."

"I'll just hug you when we exit the vehicle," Nico promised.

"Keep your hands to yourself," Keane said with a laugh, as he pulled away from the airport.

"How did they reach you? I haven't seen you in years."

"Apparently they have feelers everywhere, finding guys who are ready for a change."

"Right." Nico nodded. "I helped Miles out in the last job. Jesus, that was a nightmare."

"I hear you. This one's just … I'm not sure what it is though."

"Ryker said it could be worse than Miles's job finding that serial kidnapper who turned out to be a serial killer. But seems two jobs were pending. So we didn't get assigned that one and got the other one instead."

"Yeah, I think that's a different one," Keane said. "Ryker said a hold was on that job for a few days. So this one was more pressing, time-wise."

"Good," Nico said. "You can help me on this one, and then that horrid one can be yours. That serial killer last time was enough to finish me. Luckily the *collector* killed the serial killer. I'd have gladly taken him out myself with a quick bullet between the eyes and saved the government and all the people the pain of keeping that guy alive."

"Well, he's dead, so that's the good thing. But he got an easier and faster and less painful ending than any of those poor women. I heard the details from Miles."

"You know him too?"

"Yeah. He was part of my briefing."

"I'm not quite sure how this Mavericks system works, even after this much time," Nico said. "I was asked to come and help Miles, and, of course, I jumped at the chance."

"They didn't give me many details either on the Mavericks system," Keane said. "They were pretty closemouthed about it. But they did tell me something to go on for our op. Heard we also had some government interference on this job."

Nico snorted. "Isn't that always the kicker? I don't get why this woman was taken from her hotel."

"You should," Keane said. "She's an activist, and somebody wanted to shut her mouth."

"But you heard about the family connection?"

Keane nodded, and his face turned grim. "We need to know if it *is* connected to her kidnapping. Because, wherever that guy's name is listed, there'll be mentions of other US operatives too."

"In which case they're all compromised."

"Apparently they were all over the world, including Russia. If someone finds them, they'll get a bullet."

"Well, if we hear of anybody showing up dead or missing over the next couple days, we'll know why."

"Unless they're smart enough to spread out the killings," Keane said. "And these bad guys are getting pretty damn smart."

"Well, let's hope it's not connected," Nico said. "This could be just a simple kidnapping."

"Could be. She's also an anthropologist."

"So she studies dead societies and dead people's lifestyles," Nico said, shrugging.

"Something like that, yeah, which is also why she doesn't want the current aboriginal groups to become extinct."

"We'll all be dead here in another couple hundred years with this climate change and the political distresses," Nico said. "The world's a mess."

"Well, we can agree on that," Keane said.

Nico stared out at the huge vistas full of vivid colors all around him. The one thing about Australia that always got him was how everything seemed to be in Technicolor. The sun was super bright, and the leaves seemed greener, while the yellows seemed more yellow, and the oranges looked almost neon. "She was taken from her Sydney hotel. There were no last-minute changes to her hotel or to her flight info. So no sign of any known issues or threats facing her?"

"Not that anybody has told us," Keane said. "Not that I found online. But I researched a lot of the more recent rallies where she was in attendance. Of course, with these groups, whether she's there or not, injuries and arrests are commonplace. I remember finding an incident a few years ago at a rally she attended. A couple guys throwing bottles tried to get past security, and it got pretty ugly but nothing worse than at any music concert. Still I did run across an article about a death at another rally. Accidental of course."

"Only one? That's not as bad as what could happen at these events."

"Apparently she was distressed by it and stepped back out of the limelight. It took a lot to convince her to return to Sydney."

"She should have followed her instincts and not come here," Nico said.

"Yeah, that won't work so well," Keane said. "I've heard her speak. She's very compelling."

"Well, I listened to a couple of her videos on YouTube and also a TED talk," Nico said. "I had a long flight, and it gave me the chance to delve into her life."

"What do you think of her?"

Nico was silent for a moment and then said, "I think something started her on this pathway, and I think it was an impassioned route. Probably something to do with her first husband's death."

"I couldn't find much about his death."

"Right," Nico said. Pulling out his phone, he quickly texted Miles. **I need to know the details of her husband's death.** And he left it at that. "I think something pushed her in this direction. She's very obsessive about her subject."

"I think she's also passionate about saving the planet and saving the people. Maybe she's just that kind of a person."

"Maybe," Nico said in a more noncommittal tone. The information came in almost immediately via the chat window. Nico whistled. Then shared the info with Keane. "Makes sense now. Maybe. Apparently she lost her husband to brain cancer and he'd been big on aboriginal and environmental issues. She's more or less picked up his battle as he couldn't any longer."

"Sounds like she's carrying the torch for her dear departed hubby."

Nico nodded.

They were only a few minutes from the hotel. They pulled up, and Keane said, "Hop out. I'll be up at the room in a few minutes."

"Good enough," he said. "I'd like ten minutes of shut-eye, and then I'll need some food."

"Already arranged for food," Keane said, handing over one of the hotel cards. "Good luck getting a nap."

"Did she have the same kind of a security key card?" Nico asked. "To get in and out of her room?"

"She did, but there had been problems with it," Keane said. "They couldn't lock it properly and ended up giving her a different key that eventually worked."

"Of course there had been problems," Nico said. He hopped out of the car and grabbed his bag, then walked into the hotel and completely ignored the front desk. He headed to the elevator and up to the room. Much better nobody knew he was here. He wasn't sure what names they were registered under, if even names had been used. Often the Mavericks members operated under aliases and sometimes fake company names. But Keane got here earlier this morning, as he had been closer, and already had their room set up. Nico tossed his bag on the bed to see a gun case sitting on the floor beside it.

He opened it up and smiled. A long-range rifle and a handgun. Both already fitted with silencers. Perfect. He quickly picked up the handgun and checked that it was loaded, then put it back down again on the table beside where he would be working. Not back in the case. A gun was no good if packed away. He was one of those who never pulled it unless he needed to shoot. And, when he shot, he never intended to hurt. It was always to kill. As far as he was concerned, if he was in such a scenario where he needed a damn gun, then it was bad news, and he would take whatever way out that he needed to.

As Keane walked in, he pushed a trolley.

Nico smiled, looking at Keane, and asked, "Was it waiting out there?"

Keane shook his head. "It was just arriving."

Nico nodded, and they quickly served themselves from the trays. Steak, vegetables, and potatoes. "Looks good to me," he said. He glanced down at his watch. "Who are we working with for an update?"

"No one local," Keane said.

Nico swore. "I still don't understand that. Even with the undercover brother issue, why can't we tell the locals to just do their jobs as usual, get their help, and never mention the brother?" Still shaking his head, he brought up his laptop. Into the chat window, he typed, **We need an update for the last twelve hours. Are we working with anyone locally? Does anybody know we're here?**

None, no and no.

No update?

None yet.

Nothing from the cops?

No. But Keane was first on the scene and asked us for the basics, like to run facial recognition against all street cams focusing on the hotel and even satellite footage of our crime scene. So far we haven't seen her anywhere. Keane's been running through the traffic cams in and around the hotel, looking for anything

suspicious. Ask him for particulars.

When Nico pointed at the latest text for Keane to read, he just shook his head.

Nico swore again. **Does the hotel have a security camera on her floor?**

The two hotel security cams on her floor were covered up with something before she went missing, right before midnight on the day of her arrival, Thursday.

And uncovered, I presume, afterward?

Yes.

And, of course, nobody saw her or the person who covered up the cameras. What are the chances she's still here at the hotel?

Since we can't confirm her leaving the hotel, it's possible, Miles said in the chat window. **But I doubt they'd keep her that long at the scene of the crime. It's been twenty hours and counting since they took her.**

Nico thought about that as he cut another piece of steak.

Keane read the exchange on Nico's laptop. "Yeah, but," Keane added, "I was in the neighborhood and was already here, scouting out the place, as soon as we got word of her being missing, as soon after eight this morning as I could get here. Of course I'm not in uniform. But, because of the rally's presence in their city, the cops were everywhere. I noticed an uptick of uniforms here in this very hotel. Maybe our kidnappers didn't take that into account."

"But still, held for twenty hours at her hotel? Surely you'd want to get her spirited away as fast as possible. What's the easiest way to do that?"

Keane gave him a one-arm shrug and said, "That's easy. Take her down into the laundry room, must be in the basement, and go out that way."

Nico thought about it, then nodded, and said, "That's

almost too cinematic, but it is the simplest because how else would you move an unconscious woman? She had to be unconscious. Otherwise, no way they'd have gotten this one out of here quietly."

"No, I think she'd have been very vocal about being mistreated."

"I also didn't see any martial arts skills in her file."

"No," Keane said, "none that I know of."

Nico nodded and brought up the chat window again, then asked Miles about the laundry theory.

I'll check into it. And Miles signed off.

Nico finished his steak and jotted down more requests into the chat box. **With the laundry theory, let's get fresh eyes on this and expand our viewing area. I need a four-block radius on the video feeds from an hour before she went missing to several hours afterward up until today. Like until right now, considering she may not have left the hotel as soon as we expected,** he said. **The easiest way to take her out would have been via the laundry chutes or a laundry bin and then with a laundry truck. I'll sweep through them and have one of your people do the same. I'm sure a room-to-room search was already done by the hotel management or its own security staff, since the local cops aren't in on this investigation, but that would be pretty easy to avoid anyway.**

Shouldn't have been, Miles said. **But, yes, without you two doing the searching, then we must remember that the others wouldn't have been as experienced or as good.**

Nico didn't add anything to that and just waited. He cleaned off his plate and put it on the trolley, then waited until Keane was done and said, "We need to set up a plan of action. We're gonna look again at satellite feeds, and I'm getting more traffic cams from this area." He stopped as he looked around. "What about helicopters?" He glanced at Keane. "We need to find out if this hotel has a helicopter pad on the roof and if it's been used in the last twenty-four hours."

Keane immediately brought up his laptop and started looking. "I might just have to go downstairs to the reception desk for that."

"Go ahead. Let's see if we can find out who has the penthouses in this hotel. It could be long-term residents. It could be a standard booking. Or it could be empty. Empty is also good."

"Yeah, because *empty* to the registration desk doesn't mean it's truly empty."

Glad that he and Keane were on the same wavelength, Nico waited for the links to come in. The first one arrived, and he started in on the feeds from the nearby streets to the hotel. This batch started at seven o'clock last night—three hours before the time she initially arrived last night at this hotel—around ten o'clock. He checked, writing down notes as the vehicles came and went. It was a large hotel, and it was busy. Nothing seemed suspicious.

The second link was more street cam activity from earlier today, which gave Nico a good idea of the standard activity at this hotel. At five o'clock in the morning, the laundry trucks and delivery trucks arrived. The laundry trucks went to one bay area, while the delivery trucks went to another in a completely different section of the hotel, and cameras definitely watched them come and go.

What Nico couldn't see was what was being loaded or unloaded. They all backed up to their respective loading bays, and so he asked the chat window for a hotel camera view from inside these loading bays, only to find out there weren't any. He didn't understand that. "Why wouldn't you have a camera if you have materials being moved from your own damn hotel? Isn't that the easiest way to keep track of theft? Particularly employee theft?"

"Ours is not to wonder why," Keane said.

Nico snorted at that. "We're supposed to find answers, and yet places, like this hotel, go out of their way to stop us from getting them."

"According to the hotel manager, Charlotte used the key card to unlock her door a couple times. However, the last time she used her key, she supposedly held the door open—probably for her night visitor or her friend who she was with—while she grabbed something and left."

Nico stopped and thought about that. "I suppose that would work. What about her luggage?"

"After her coworker reported Charlotte as missing to both the hotel and the local authorities, the hotel's cleaning crew was ordered to stay away from that room. However, the manager did open the door and looked inside, probably to see if any damage was done to the room or to see if she was there, dead or alive. Regardless he says her belongings were not visible, seemingly all gone."

"Which goes along with the kidnapping theory."

Keane nodded. "Of course the kidnapper will take every-thing he can."

"I want to start there," Nico said. "I want to get into her room."

"I was ordered away from that floor, so nobody pegged me as interested in this matter, so I've been mostly watching the lobby and the loading bay for anything suspicious when not going through the street cam footage. I've been told her room has been cordoned off."

"Good," he said. "That'll mean that most people can't get in and mess up my crime scene. What floor?"

Keane checked his notes. "She's on the sixth floor on our side of the building. You want to go from inside or out?"

"If her lock is registered, then somebody will know if we go in."

"Unless the hotel's management or security or household staff are allowed back in there, but I haven't heard any update on that. So we'll presume that room is not to be disturbed by the hotel personnel."

"We'll have to go in from the outside," Nico said. Then he headed out on the balcony and took a look up. "It would be easier if we had police cooperation. But, if we have to stay undercover because of her brother, well, … we climb up, or we hinder the hall security cameras again and climb over one balcony."

"There's no help for it," Keane said. "These are our options."

Nico nodded. "I presume the room numbers align for each floor. So our room isn't in a straight line to hers. However, if we disable the hall cameras long enough to get into one of the rooms next door to hers, then we'll use the neighboring balcony to enter her room, avoiding the whole key card issue. So we need to find out who's in the rooms beside her and go in from one of those, if at all possible. These balconies aren't the easiest to get in and out of, which I'm happy to see. The span's too long for a jump or even a temporary walkway, but we can use ropes to get from one to the other." He went back to his bag and brought out what he had, then said, "Not that I came too well-equipped for skyscraper climbing." He had several carabiners and some rope with him but not enough.

"I've got a big bag of gear," Keane said, "one full of tactical equipment." He brought it out of the closet and dumped it onto the carpet. They quickly sorted through the equipment, and Nico nodded with satisfaction.

"You know what? We'll be okay to do this. Let's get going now. First thing is to check where she was taken from, and then we'll come back and fill in the rest of the details. We have to at least have a starting point."

THE ROUGH COTTON band tied too tightly around Charlotte Ankerby's mouth bit into the sides of her gums, and she knew she was bleeding. Unconsciousness was a gift her kidnappers weren't prepared to give her. And that didn't bode well for her end result. She could see their faces and hear their conversations, yet she didn't know who they were and neither were they giving much away. But the fact that they weren't hiding themselves meant they didn't care if she saw them or not, so either they would be dead soon or she would be dead soon, and she knew it would most likely be her. They'd taken her phone and left her in three-quarter length jeans, a T-shirt, and slip-on sandals on her feet.

They'd caught her as she had unlocked her door to return to her hotel room. She'd been just so tired that she hadn't even recognized when the men came upon her. She had just pulled open her hotel room door when they snagged her. They'd shoved her inside, subdued her, then quickly picked her up and her luggage, and took her back out again. All before the door closed. She figured they must have jammed it with something somehow, but she didn't know.

Now here she was, lying in the back of a large vehicle of some kind. Maybe a refrigerator truck? She had no clue, but she was cold, and she was tired. She was beyond tired, and four of them sat at the end of the large five-ton truck, talking. Two of them were smoking and filling the back of the truck with that pungent odor that she couldn't stand. Nobody had been happier than she was when her city passed the no-smoking-in-public ban. But, in places like this, nobody gave a shit. She coughed several more times, trying to free her lungs of that smoke. One of the men laughed at her, but the other guy said, "Jesus Christ, I wish you'd stop smoking in here. There's no air."

"Shut the fuck up," the smoker replied.

She could put voices to their faces. She just didn't know why they were doing this.

She'd been warned several times that her activism would get her in trouble, but she seemed compelled to keep doing what she was doing. It had occurred to her that maybe she would be better off to put her words onto paper and to write books that incited people to reconsider their actions and to rethink their places in this world. And she'd made a concert-ed effort in that direction.

Australia had never been part of her new plans, until she had been coerced to go. She'd been so adamant against coming. She was tired and worn out from her schedule, wanting to just curl up in her cave. But the organizers had already promoted her presence here, saying that, due to a communication mix-up, she had to honor it. It was a long trip from California to Sydney, and she felt she had no choice.

However, she should have stuck to her guns and said that she had never agreed to come. It was their problem and not hers, and what a crappy way to force people to show up for their event by promoting them and then saying it was their fault? She even wondered now if the organizers weren't part of her kidnapping.

After a lot of emails back and forth, she'd gotten quite disgruntled and unhappy over being pressured to show up for something she hadn't agreed to. She knew she'd been deceived, and, by showing up, the con had worked, and that just made her even angrier because look at where she was now. She'd also come alone instead of with her assistant, Maggie. Considering Charlotte's circumstances, she was grateful for that, except that they would have stayed in the room together, and maybe her assistant could have put out the word. On the other hand, her assistant would likely be lying in this truck beside her.

Charlotte was happy Maggie had stayed home. She was a good person; she didn't need this. She had a bum knee and lots of stomach issues. She was also on the back side of sixty and had already slid well into her grandmotherly type of role, whereas Charlotte herself had just crossed over the thirty-three-year-old mark, with no children or even a boyfriend or future husband in sight.

And maybe that was her fault. When Rowe had died, she hadn't wanted to try marriage again. She'd been a devoted wife, but he had gotten ill very soon after their marriage. Medical bills had been a huge issue, and they couldn't afford the best in the way of treatment. The bank had offered a loan to help, but Rowe needed specialized treatment for a particular brain cancer and not enough funds were coming in their direction, not even with a bank loan.

So, instead of being a happy wife, starting a family, and becoming a mother, she'd ended up as an overly tired and very inexperienced nursemaid. She had done so willingly, but it had taken its toll on her. By the time Rowe had passed away, his regrets and apology still in her ears, she'd been so exhausted that it had been almost a relief. And, of course, the guilt had eaten away at her, keeping her stuck in the same time and place mentally for a lot longer than it should have.

He had died six years ago, and she'd still not moved on. Maybe it was out of guilt because she hadn't been able to save him. She was an anthropologist and had always loved cultures that had come and gone before her. After Rowe's death she'd finally turned her attention to bringing awareness to the current world and how much change was needed. She'd known that her time being an activist was over and that she would return to writing books that would hopefully open up people's eyes and make them think and listen a little more.

As the planet slid into a climate crisis, she understood on a more global scale just how much people were damaging Mother Earth and its inhabitants. It was no longer just about the cultures of the people who had gone before them but it was also about the cultures of today who were inhaling the resources without care, multiplying and breeding well past the point of capacity, so that the planet itself was under siege.

She knew if she even started writing books on this subject that, for every two people in front of her, one would think she was a fool, and the other would call her a saint. That's how divided the people were, particularly in her own country. It made her sad. But, in a way, she was also glad she wasn't bringing children into this. She couldn't even guarantee the planet would be here in eighty or ninety years to see any of her own children grow up. Of course she'd be long gone by then, but what kind of an attitude was that to take? Take what you wanted and then die? That wasn't her style.

But this? ... Her future might be only a byline in a newspaper article and then buried, gone—forgotten. How sad.

She glanced around again at the four walls of the truck and the men down at the one end, playing cards. At least the one guy had put out his cigarette. The other one though? Looked like the tip of his cigarette hung with an inch of ash still attached to the end of the filter. But then she didn't even know if he inhaled his cigarettes or if it was just more of a habit to light them. He'd live longer if he gave it up, but she'd be happy if he'd drop dead right now.

She shifted and moaned at her aching arms and legs. They were at least tied in front of her with duct tape, so she could roll onto her back and stretch her shoulders ever-so-slightly, but the band around her mouth was painfully tight. Her throat was dry, and she could hardly even swallow anymore. She kept trying to work the saliva in her throat to stop her from choking on the fibers she inhaled, but, as soon as her mouth got completely dry, it's almost like she'd spasm, trying to get liquid across her raw tissues.

She couldn't imagine being out in the desert for three or four days and still surviving. This had only been overnight and beyond that into today, for however many hours—at least from what she could determine without a watch or a window—and she was in agony. With any luck, somebody had reported her missing, and a full investigation would be done.

But she also knew that half of the people would probably consider it a good thing to have her gone. She hated to think that that's how the world would remember her. And yet she knew that she'd stirred some people in the right way. If that's all that she could do, then that's all she could do.

CHAPTER 2

CHARLOTTE TRIED TO bring up Rowe's face in her mind, to see that glimpse of the man she'd loved so much. He'd been such a different personality at the end of his illness though. The drugs had changed him and his body. He had suffered terribly from the disease and the chemo and the medications. He'd reacted almost worse to the medications. He'd finally been put into a hospice, and she'd been at his side right to the end.

Every once in a while though, he'd be attacked by his own anger at his situation, and it would hit him hard, and he'd lash out at her because she was still young and healthy. She tried to forgive him for those times, realizing it was just his circumstances talking, his own rage at his own inability to change his situation at the time.

But, when she'd walked out those hospice doors on that last day, she'd gotten into her vehicle, and she cried and cried and cried. Partly for the loss of the Rowe she knew but also partly for relief because she hadn't thought she could make it one more day with the angry version of him.

Her own body had been right on the edge of exhaustion. Her mind and emotions had been stretched so thin, and yet to still have him berate her for being allowed to live? She knew death hit everybody differently, and the one thing she could hope for herself was that she would walk through those pearly gates kicking and screaming right to the end, so that she could enjoy every last moment.

But then, when faced with no other recourse, she'd accept that destination and take that final step forward bravely. What she really didn't want was to turn around and blame those around her for her impending death—*if* she was lucky enough to have anybody around her at the end of her life. She was an orphan, having spent the latter part of her childhood and most of her teen years in foster care, hating every day of it, yet had been old enough to understand that life wouldn't get any better unless she made it better herself.

As soon as she could, she had left the foster care system.

But something about meeting Rowe and going through everything she had with him felt like she needed a cause. Some form of action that she could take to make it seem like she was doing something. That she'd picked up her husband's causes and that had been how she'd started but they'd quickly become her own. Watching him going through what he had … she'd been helpless to do anything but be there for him. Support him emotionally … Taking up his causes had given her a voice. She finally had to open up and to say all that she could say because, all through his illness, she hadn't been able to tell him how she felt about his life. Her life. What their life had become. About his treatment. About the ramifications of his disease and how badly it had ravaged him.

She'd written down everything that she could in order to drain those emotions and those thoughts from her system, so she didn't turn on him when she got up in the middle of the night and once again changed the soiled bedding for a man who held so much hatred. She never blamed him. How could she? He was just devastated by what the disease had done to his body. If anyone was more ashamed and humiliated, it's that a man, so big and strong, had fallen down to be nothing more than an organic waste.

They both cried at times, holding each other close, and she'd wanted to rail and scream at cancer, and at this stupid man that could mean so much, and yet said so little about what was eating away at him. She'd gone through so much torment by the time of his death—both her own emotional distress and that caused by Rowe when in one of his rages—that she'd quickly buried herself in her studies, finished her education, got involved in her causes in a big way plus she started writing more as a necessity than anything because of her ever-worrying guilt.

Guilt that she could have done one more thing for him. That she *should* have done one more thing for him and yet hadn't been able to or couldn't do more because nothing more could be done. As she lay here on her back, she whispered in her mind, *I'm coming, Rowe. I'm not sure how far away I am, but I'll be there sooner than expected.*

And she closed her eyes and sank back into a restless sleep, tears drying on her cheeks.

NICO DOUBLE-CHECKED THE hotel's security camera feeds but there were no recordings from that hallway leading to her room on the night Charlotte had been taken.

Now physically on her floor, he came up behind a second security camera and carefully tossed a towel up on the top, just like he did for the first camera, catching it and blocking it out immediately. And, with that, he and Keane donned gloves and moved to the room on the other side of

Charlotte's. Having checked the hotel's register, he knew this one was empty. He took a moment to open the door, swiping one of the master keys he had taken from a maid's uniform hanging atop a cart outside in the hallway. He wasn't sure where the maid went, but it had been convenient, so he'd taken advantage of it. He even wondered exactly why the maid wasn't here.

As he went in, Keane followed him, and they quickly closed the door and walked out onto the balcony. Then they opened up their gear and used a rope and an anchor and quickly hooked on to the other railing, which was just a little too far to span otherwise. And, with a short rope, they quickly crossed over and jumped to the other side. He left the rope there in case he needed to make a fast getaway. He entered in through the locked balcony doors, quickly picking the lock and popping inside.

He did a search around the room. The bed hadn't been disturbed, yet a glass had been unwrapped and used in the bathroom. She hadn't touched the minibar, and no obvious belongings were left behind. He bent to look under the bed but found nothing there either. Frowning, he checked around and wondered if any fingerprints or something forensic had been left behind. Had the hotel security team even checked? He quickly pulled out his phone and asked.

The hotel security staff assured me that they're on it.

Nobody's been here, from what I can see, other than our victim and her kidnappers. And the cops have not been here. I saw no crime scene tape at the door and no fingerprint dust in this room.

Are you sure you're in the right room?

Six hundred twelve?

Yes.

The locals have done nothing?

Maybe they think they are to back off completely on investigating this one.

Maybe, he said, **but that's not good. It's been almost a full day already.**

Nico did a quick search, going into the closet, checking everything, including the drawers. The bottom drawer held pants, the second held shirts, and the top held underwear, socks, bras. He found no luggage here, so, if she hadn't unpacked all her luggage, when the kidnappers grabbed her and her bags, the kidnappers thought they had taken it all. But underneath her lingerie were her return tickets and passport. He quickly mentioned that to his team.

Take it all, Miles said. **You can leave the clothing if you want, but she'll need the passport to get herself into the country.**

Is it safe to disrupt the crime scene, do you think?

We need to get her first, and then we need to get her out of there. Papers will make it easier to get her back home again.

Not to mention we have some US military help, correct?

Navy for sure, Miles said with a thumbs-up emoji.

Nico quickly pulled out the passport and the paperwork, then glanced at it and tucked it into his shirt pocket. He went through the rest, wondering if he should pack up the clothing. Noting how very little was here, she must have come for just a couple days. On a whim, he rolled it all up into a tight ball and stuffed it into the back of his tactical bag. And then, just like that, he and Keane were out crossing between balconies again, then exited the other hotel room and reentered the hotel hallway.

As he walked past, he removed the towels from the two

security cams, and they disappeared into the stairwell and back to their room, removing their gloves and pocketing them as they went. As he got in, he swore, "That was a complete waste."

"Not really," Keane said. "We know she didn't leave on her own if she didn't take her passport."

He had to give him a plus on that one. "But we took evidence from the local cops. Except they don't seem to be doing their jobs."

"I'm sure our guys will tell them when necessary."

Nico sat down and pulled out the paperwork, then went through her passport. Nothing different here. He looked at the rest of the stack of papers. Some of it appeared to be part of her speech for the keynote talk, while other sheets appeared to be notes of some kind, maybe for a book. They seemed to be more amusing anecdotes or sad journal entries. And she had a stack of one-hundred-dollar bills as well. He frowned. "These are still in US dollars. She didn't even convert to Australian dollars."

"No time maybe," Keane said.

"Or she was going somewhere else."

"Or she needed it for something. Could even be that's her level of comfort zone though."

"And yet we found no purse," he said thoughtfully.

"So, she didn't keep her passport in her purse or this kind of money there either."

The two men looked at each other and frowned.

"Either she expected a problem or just assumed there could be one." Nico quickly folded everything together, then added the papers and the documents to the rest of her things stashed in his bag. It still didn't help them at all in locating her, although it would make getting her back into the country easier. He sat down with the video feeds and checked all the entrances and exits.

At that point in time, Keane crowed. "Okay, so we have a helicopter that arrived not the night she was taken but after the kidnapping."

Instantly Nico focused on his friend. "When did it leave?"

Keane kept tapping away on his keyboard and then said, "It hasn't yet."

Ever so slowly, the two men stared at each other.

"What are the chances that that's how she's getting out of here? That the pilot stayed at the hotel overnight? Or was he paid to deliver it and not paid to wait around?" asked Nico.

"I still like the laundry idea for sneaking her from her room to the basement and then out on some truck," Keane admitted. "But having a helicopter would be way better for the kidnappers to escape."

"Did the hotel security team search all the kitchens and laundry rooms too?"

"Apparently, yes."

Nico sat back and thought about it. "Okay. If she's not in the hotel, then they won't use the helicopter, will they?"

"They'd have to bring her back in again in order to get her up to the helicopter, and that would be dangerous."

"The helicopter being here makes me think Charlotte has to be here too. So the kidnappers must have her hidden somewhere that the hotel's security people couldn't find her."

"Also don't you think that, even if they had her hidden in the hotel, they would have already moved the helicopter as soon as possible?"

"Unless there was a hitch in those plans," Nico said thoughtfully. "Anyway, check who owns the helicopter and what its plans are."

"I'm digging into that. Plus I have something on the two penthouses in this hotel. We've got a businessman staying in one, and the other has an ongoing relationship with an import-export company."

At that, Nico rolled his eyes. Because import and export covered everything from drugs to cars to women. And probably 90 percent of them were legit, but the ones that weren't gave everything else in that whole business arena a bad name. "Let's see if there's a pilot around that we can talk to."

"On it."

Nico continued studying all the traffic cameras, looking to see if she'd been smuggled out another way. He kept rubbing his eyes as the vehicles swam on the screen in front of him. It was a stupid system where he had to keep watch on multitudes of vehicles all at the same time. "If they had planned to take the helicopter, they would have stayed in the hotel building. Or at least nearby."

"Makes sense. But, if they were taking her out in a delivery truck, they would have stashed her until the next one was scheduled."

"But lots of deliveries were moving all through the night and into the morning. They only needed a place to store her for a few hours, and then they could easily have moved her out in the next laundry or food truck or any other truck."

"I agree with that," Keane said. "So, if they've taken Charlotte from this hotel, what we need are all the names of all the staff who worked in the kitchen and in the unloading bays and in the laundry and see how many of them are still at work today."

Nico quickly asked his chat window support for all the related information. Unfortunately this was a huge hotel, and, by the time he got the staff list, he groaned. "Thirty names to check here."

"Let's start knocking them off then. We don't have the luxury of time here, so let's go by the standard profiling. Cross off anybody who's married with family here. Anybody who's been on staff for a year or more."

So, with the chat's help, they narrowed the list from that point down to those who were making decent money, then to a list of single males of any age who hadn't been at the hotel for very long. Less than three months was the time frame they put on that and then checked who would normally have worked today but didn't show up. Two names came up. Nico quickly twisted the laptop around and said, "Just these two."

"Let's find addresses and go check them out."

That took another three minutes. By the time they had those, they were already fully armed and heading outside. "Time to have a talk with those guys, huh?"

"Depending on what's going on," Keane said, "I'm not too sure if these guys will be around to talk to."

"If they're smart, they would have gone with the rest of the crew."

"Maybe, and maybe they're in the way."

"Depends if they've done this before or if this is a steady operation."

"Hope you're not bringing up sex workers or white slavery," Keane said. "That's the last thing I want to deal with."

"I hear you," Nico said. "But there could be only so many scenarios. Something like this has four likely options."

"Humanity is a sick place," Keane said. "There are as many options in this world as you can possibly think of. The trouble is, we can only think of so many, hindered by our apparent lack of evil intent, until a new scenario comes up. Then we realize how logical it is, from a malevolent point of view."

The two men exited in the same vehicle and pulled out into the night, just about twenty-one hours since she'd gone missing.

"I still think that, if they were smart," Keane said, "they'd have taken her a long way away by now."

"If they were smart, they wouldn't have done this in the first place," Nico said. "At least not here, not in a public place. Would have been much easier to have run her vehicle off the road and taken her then."

"She didn't drive. At least not here. She took cabs."

"Has anybody checked with the cab companies to make sure she didn't get a ride somewhere?"

"The team is on it but so far nothing has turned up," Keane said.

Since Nico wasn't driving, he sent the request for more information. One thing about jobs like this was their never-ending thirst for answers. And you never knew what you didn't know until it popped up.

They hit the first employee's address. It was an apartment in a middle-income neighborhood. Donning another pair of disposable gloves, Nico and Keane checked the area before leaving their car.

Nico picked the locks and defined this place as *empty cold*, as if nobody had lived here in a while. But food was in the fridge. An air of desolation surrounded the place, and, despite the presence of food, the furniture looked cold, uncomfortable. Nico looked over at Keane and said, "Doesn't feel like somebody's been here for a few days."

"No, it doesn't."

They did a quick sweep. Clothes were in the dressers, laundry in the hamper, and shampoo in the bathroom. "So he's planning on coming back," Nico said. "He's just not here at the moment. Interesting."

They slipped out the back, locking it up like it had been, and returned to their vehicle, not bothering to take off their gloves just yet. After typing in the second employee's address into their vehicle's GPS, they headed out. When they got to his place, they found a small bungalow nestled in a block of similar-looking houses. It was a little bit better secured with bolts and a lock, but, even with that, they got in easily enough.

As soon as they entered through the back door though, they both stopped and froze.

The smell …

"Shit," Nico said, his heart sinking. "This is not good."

"We need to confirm though," Keane said.

Silently they quickly went in with handguns out and at the ready. They swept through the small bedroom. Using flashlights, they held the light up to study the body on the bed, atop the covers, fully dressed, with one bullet to the head.

"I wonder if this is one of our two hotel workers," Nico said. He quickly took a photo of his face and sent it in for Miles to identify.

"It's hard to see in this light. The photo on the file wasn't very current."

"I know." Just then Nico turned and headed to the bathroom. "And here's a second one," he called out. "And I recognize this one. These are our two missing employees."

The two men exchanged hard looks, and Nico quickly told Miles about the newest update. Then he pocketed his phone, completed a full search of the house, looking for anything that would lead them to Charlotte or to find out why the kidnappers would have taken out these two local men. "Either they were loose ends or they caused trouble," Nico said. "Or the other kidnappers are increasing profits for the job by reducing the number of ways the money needed to be split."

"You know what? I'm almost tempted to believe the last one. It doesn't make any sense that they would be cleaning up, unless they're planning on killing Charlotte. And, with that damn helo on the roof, I don't think she's dead. Not at this point anyway."

"And yet," Nico stated, "there's got to be another reason to kill her, not just because she's an activist."

"You're right," he said. "She didn't have that big a voice in that community. It's not like she made national head-lines."

"She wasn't targeting a particular company or industry either," Nico continued, "so it's not like some big monopoly would be after her."

"And that takes us back to the brother issue."

Both men were silent and grim as they moved from room to room. In the kitchen in one drawer full of odds and ends they pulled out a notepad. A few names were written on it. Nico tapped the top name and said, "That's the second DB in the bathroom." They quickly tore off the top list and checked for more. Nico took a photo of the list, then sent it to Miles. **These names, check them out.**

"Why would he have that list here?" Keane asked, studying it.

"Hard to say but maybe it was early on, when they first started working together, and he wanted to know who the team members were."

"Well, I know I wouldn't work solo with somebody if I didn't know who they were," Keane said.

"Yet we've all worked with teams where we didn't know some of the guys," Nico said. "We might have had a first name or a second name, but, chances are, those aren't the names that their mothers knew them by."

"Yeah, but we *knew* who they were," Keane said with a half smile. "We knew who they were inside. Otherwise we wouldn't be working with them."

"Agreed," Nico said. Then, after a complete search of the home, the two of them turned and looked at each other. "Now to check the bodies," Nico said. A couple empty grocery bags were on the counter. He quickly grabbed them both, and they returned to the first body. Keane followed. There, Nico pulled out the first DB's wallet and dropped it inside one plastic bag and handed that to Keane, while Nico checked the rest of his pockets, doing as well as he could to not move the body. Considering the deceased was on his back, it was just a case of lifting up one side to make sure that each pocket was freed up.

With all the pockets turned inside out, and the cell phone taken, he handed everything over to add to the first bag Keane held, and then both men went to the second body. This one had a cell phone, a wallet and loose change too, but nothing else. That all went into the second grocery bag. In the kitchen, they quickly went through the wallets, looking for anything helpful. They photographed everything and then returned the wallets to the bodies. "The cops need the cell phones too," Keane noted.

"Agreed. Sending everything on these to ours." Nico pulled out a small device and hooked it up to each of the hotel workers' cell phones and quickly downloaded as much as he could; then he popped out the sim card and replaced it with another one.

"You always walk around with sim cards?" Keane asked.

"Standard issue in my to-go bag now," Nico said.

Keane shrugged and said, "If you say so."

And then they turned and walked out, making sure they left no fingerprints on the doors either, taking off and pocketing their disposable gloves once outside. Back in their vehicle, this time Nico took over the driving as they headed toward the hotel. His phone rang, and he tossed it to Keane. "It'll be Miles."

"Miles, what's up?"

"I've arranged for an anonymous caller to alert the local cops about the two DBs you found. Both men have records, but it's all recent. Like in the last two to three months. Otherwise they're both clean, and they both worked only at the hotel. Both were hired three months ago, after they had attended a job fair, and were hired on the spot. Didn't appear to have any prior connection before working together at the hotel."

"Well, they moved into a really ugly sideline of life."

"Makes me wonder if somebody else at the hotel might have recruited them."

"Money is a great motivator," Nico said to Miles, the phone now on Speaker mode. "If you think about it, these are both young men, looking to make something out of their life or to have a different life instead of this drudgery of a nine-to-five, working in the laundry room of a big hotel. If they were offered big money, chances are they jumped at it and didn't even ask questions."

"Or they asked too many questions," Keane said with a look over at Nico.

Nico turned the corner up ahead and pulled into the hotel's underground parking lot. "That's true too," he admitted. "What we need to know is if our two DBs were friendly with anybody else who worked at the hotel."

Keane clicked away on his phone, thankful to have a copy of the dead kidnappers' contacts sent to him as well. "Checking the contacts on our two DBs. Ah-ha. Charles Huntington. He's on shift right now, and he's due off in half an hour."

"Laundry?" Nico asked.

"Loading and unloading for the trucks and sorting and restocking the shelves," Miles explained.

"Okay. Do you have a photo, Miles?" Nico asked. "We'll have to come in through the laundry area, find him, and talk to him."

"Sending you a photo now. You do that and just be quiet about it then," Miles said. "There's a good chance he won't be pleased about speaking to the authorities."

"Rap sheet?" Keane asked.

"Yes. Breaking and entering," Miles said.

"Good enough," Keane said. "We won't go in as cops though. Maybe as some local hustle, looking to see if he's interested in some jobs."

"Or maybe as a local hustler who knows he's already involved in a job," Nico corrected. Grim, he added, "Chances are, he is in over his head."

"Let's go find out."

CHAPTER 3

C HARLOTTE HAD BEEN moved from the truck to another laundry cart. Like, what the hell was with that? She was being pushed even now down a hallway. She had no idea why all kinds of discussions were going on in front of her, but one of those was about a helicopter. She wondered exactly who and what was going by helicopter because, if it was her, that wasn't good news. That would mean she had pissed off somebody really big. She groaned silently.

She wanted the companies to do more, and she wanted the governments to do more. But what she really wanted most was for the world to wake up and to pay attention. To everything—the people, the animals, the climate, and the planet. But, of course, everybody was addicted to their instant conveniences and were happy to stick their heads in the sand about any future generations' problems and make it a *not me* problem. She shifted uneasily in the bottom of the bag only to have the top of her head smacked, hard. "Don't move."

She took several deep calming breaths. She was covered with laundry and hadn't really thought anybody would notice, but maybe it made the bag itself move. She stuck a finger along the edge and waggled it. Could somebody else see it? But she did not want the man pushing her to know.

Using her feet, she set up a slight rhythm on the end of

the laundry cart. At least the guy pushing her wouldn't see that. And, with the swaying as they moved forward, it should cover her movements. So far, she hadn't even heard anybody in the hallway. How did that work? Sure, it was probably late at night again, at least by her estimation, but she was losing track of time. They've given her several bathroom breaks, but somebody stood guard each time, watching her.

The first time it made her feel really icky. The second time had been a matter of urgency and she'd been just too damn grateful that she hadn't worried as much about them watching her. She had muttered *Pervert* as he walked past though and had been cuffed on the side of the head for that comment. Still, it hadn't beaten her spirits down too badly.

As long as they were on the move, surely somebody, anybody might see them by chance. The cart jolted as it took a sudden turn. She listened intently, and, sure enough, she heard footsteps up ahead. She didn't know if it was just one person or not. She also didn't know if that person would help her or if it was somebody meeting this guy.

"Hey, you still on duty?"

"Last load," said the guy pushing her cart.

"Man, it's late for you."

"I know, right? But the place is a nuthouse."

"If only I had a share of the money that this hotel was pulling in," the new guy said enviously. His footsteps continued to walk on past ever-so-slightly.

She again used her foot to make it look like something moved inside the cart, but he hadn't even seemed to notice. She sank back, feeling hot tears in her eyes. Something in that new voice had her desperate to try to jump out though. But then, if it got her killed, what good would that do? And then suddenly she heard the voice call out, "Hey, by the way, where are you taking that laundry hamper to?"

"It's going up to the penthouse. Why?" asked the guy pushing her. She could hear the tension running through his voice like a coiled wire stretched too tight.

"I didn't think that was part of your job."

"What the hell do you know about my job?" the guy said defensively.

"Well, for one, the penthouse doesn't get laundry carts like that," the guy said in a dry tone. "And, for another, you're well past your shift."

"I'm not. I still have ten minutes left."

"Yeah, well, let me see what's inside your laundry cart."

"What the hell do you care, man?"

"I care," he said, "so just shut it and let me see."

"It's fucking laundry. But sure, if you're into laundry, go for it. Here. Come on over and take a look."

If the guy bent over, she knew what would happen. Her kidnapper would hit this poor person if she didn't do something. She struggled to move underneath the laundry, but it seemed to be at the same time that they were lifting up laundry above her. She screamed behind her gag, a sound that she swore was yelling at top decibels but came out as a muted moan.

And then she heard the new guy say, "Hey, what the hell is this?"

Her kidnapper said, "You fucking asshole, get out of my business."

She heard a blow hit. She tried to sit up and push off all the laundry that had been put on top of her. She felt some of it giving way. She reached for the edge of the hamper and tried to stand, sending the rest of the laundry all over the floor. She fell over the side of the hamper to the floor, completely caught up in the laundry.

As the two men fought, she scrambled to stand, when suddenly somebody picked her up and threw her over his shoulder, and she was carried down the hallway. She tried to scream and wiggle free but then she was in an elevator. She moaned and fought, her body struggling hard as she tried to head-bang him away.

Then she was set on her feet, and the binding around her mouth was ripped free, and a voice asked, "Are you Charlotte?"

She nodded, staring in the dimly lit elevator to see who it was. She felt a little reassured that the doors to the elevator remained open.

"You're safe now," he said.

She stared up, her gaze widening. "Who are you?" she whispered.

"My name is Nico. My partner's attacking your kidnapper right now."

She shook her head and frantically said, "He's only one of four. You have to help him."

"Help my buddy? No, somebody needs to help your kidnapper," he said. Just then another man came into the elevator, pushing the laundry cart.

As she stared down, her kidnapper was facing up, but he was unconscious. "Is he dead?" she whispered.

The new arrival just grinned and shook his head, pushing a button on the elevator to close the doors and to get it moving now.

As she stood here, shivering and trembling at the sudden change of her circumstances, she said, "If you don't clean up all that laundry out there, somebody'll notice."

"Yeah. They'll notice and blame him."

Before she could process it, her arms were separated from her bindings. She groaned as Nico dropped her arms gently to her side. She shuddered with pain, but her rescuer rubbed the top of each of her arms all the way down to her hands. She looked to see the knife he'd used to separate the duct tape. She whispered, "Thank you. I thought my arms had died."

"No problem. It's always rough at first, when trying to get the blood flowing again," he said, a note of apology in his voice. "Take the rest of the bindings off while I cut your feet apart." He quickly separated the tape at her ankles and ripped it off. She'd been wearing slip-on sandals and Capri jeans, so the duct tape had left a raw red band on her skin. But she barely felt it with all the blood rushing to her extremities. Just being upright made her a bit dizzy. She huddled against the corner as she slowly tried to get the rest of duct tape off her wrists.

When he straightened and looked at her, he said, "I'm sorry. It'll hurt, but it's much better this way." And he grabbed one hand, then he grabbed her wrist, and he just ripped. She cried out in pain, but he did it again. She stared up at him, her eyes wounded and her mouth open, knowing that the odd keening sound was coming from her, but she was unable to stop it.

Immediately he pulled her into his arms and just held her close. "It's okay. You're safe now."

She collapsed against him, tears pouring down her cheeks. "Why did they choose me?" she whispered. "Why me?"

"We're trying to figure that out," he said. "Maybe when he wakes up, he'll have a few answers for us."

"Aren't you taking him to the police?"

"Nah," the second guy said. "Don't really feel like help-ing the police out on this one."

She stared up at him, a little nervous and confused. "Are you not the police?"

The man shook his head. "No," he said, "but you're safe with us."

She bit her bottom lip. "Am I though? I'm not exactly sure about that."

"Well, you're no longer tied up, and we've taken out your kidnapper, so maybe you could rethink that."

She blinked slightly, trying to figure out just what had happened. "If you're not the police," she said, her voice gaining in strength, "who are you?"

"We're military, Special Ops," the first guy said. "US Navy. And we came here to collect you."

She stared at him. "Okay," she said slowly. "But you're a long way from home."

"That's quite true," he said, handing her a burner phone. "Should we get separated, use only this phone to communi-cate with only me. My number's the only one in the Contacts list."

She numbly stuck the phone in her jeans pocket, frown-ing.

Just then the elevator came to a stop, and one guy backed out, pulling his laundry cart with her kidnapper still in it. The other one grabbed her arm, following his partner, and said, "Come on. Let's go."

She was still half wrapped up against him but stumbled along. Her legs were moving but not as well as they should have been. Her hands were killing her. She cradled both of her sore wrists up against her chest as he wrapped an arm around her and led her to a hotel room. They all entered and then locked the door behind them.

Once inside, she looked around and said, "Are we safe here?"

"Maybe," he said opening a small fridge and pulling out a bottle of water. He uncapped it and handed it to her. "At least we're hoping so."

After a long drink, she sagged on the bed, even as the other guy pulled up her kidnapper and dragged him to a chair in the little kitchenette area, then sat him down. They quickly tied him to the chair and left him unconscious but sitting. She watched everything happening around her as if it were a movie, as if she weren't really connected. She kept telling her brain to figure this out and to snap out of whatever fugue she was in. But it wasn't working.

"If you're not cops," she said, "shouldn't you at least contact them?"

"We will as soon as we know what's going on here."

"This guy and three others kidnapped me," she whispered. "I had just returned to my hotel room, had unlocked my door, and they snatched me up. I didn't even get a chance to step inside. They went in, grabbed my bags to make it look like I had gone or something, and then they took me and left."

"Right," the first guy said. "And you are Charlotte Ankerby, correct?"

She nodded slowly. "And who are you?"

He quickly reintroduced himself and said, "Just call me Nico."

"Nico, how did you know where I was?"

"Well, we figured that you were still in the hotel. Then narrowed it down to the laundry area in the basement or the helicopter on the roof."

"It was both," she said. "I don't understand the helicopter part, but I heard the kidnappers talking about it."

"In that case," Nico said, "one of us needs to disappear really fast."

He stood up but the other guy—Keane, she thought his name was—stood and said, "I'll go. You keep an eye on these two." And he disappeared out the door.

She looked back at Nico. "Where's he going?"

"To the rooftop. He'll see if you were to be taken to the helicopter waiting up there."

"That's not a good thing to think about, but I did wonder."

"What can you tell me about the other men with this guy?"

"The truck was too smoky," she said. "And unfortunately that was the biggest thing I remember about them."

"Were they young or old?"

"Two were young," she said. "As in very young. I didn't know who they were or anything about them. But they were happy to be doing this, as if this was something that they hadn't really expected to do, and they were now part of the in-group."

He brought out his cell phone and held up a picture. "Is this one of them?"

She looked at it, frowned, and nodded. "Yes, it is. But …?"

"It's him," he said. "Only he's dead. He was shot sometime in the last twenty-four hours."

She frowned. "I can't really tell you when, but, the last time I saw him, they were inside the big truck where I was held. Two men were smoking at the time, and all four of them were playing cards. This unconscious guy's one of them. And the guy on your phone is one of the other ones."

"Is he one of the ones who smoked?"

She nodded. "Yes, but I don't know if the other kid did too."

He flicked through his phone again and brought up another photo.

She turned her head away. "God. Is he dead too?"

"Sorry, but that's the better of the two photos I have of him. And, yes, this kid's dead. Is he one of the four who you saw?"

"Yes," she said. "So two are dead, and now there's this guy, and I don't know where the other guy is."

"Well, we need to find him," Nico said. "We have a few questions we want to ask him."

She stared at him, confused. "About me?" she asked hesitantly. A groan from the man tied to the chair interrupted their conversation. She looked over at Nico and said, "Is it wrong that I want to go over there and kick the shit out of him?"

Nico laughed. "I think that's a very normal and healthy reaction. Except I can't let you do it."

"And I don't think I'd like myself afterward either," she said. "But to think that he kidnapped me from my hotel room and kept me locked up for twenty-four hours or longer? By the way, what day and time is it?"

"Sydney time, it's Friday, almost midnight. If you were taken about eleven-thirty p.m. Thursday, then they held you for approximately twenty-five hours. So was there anything important that you would miss in those hours?" he asked casually, but she got the distinct impression that her answer was important.

She looked up at him and blinked. "Yes. I was supposed

to give a speech."

He turned ever-so-slowly and looked at her. "Is that the reason you think you were kidnapped? Were they intending to silence you?"

She stared back at him and blinked, but her mind churned on the idea. "Maybe? I was pretty unhappy with the way the organizers had set this up."

"Maybe you'd better tell me about that before this guy wakes up, so I know what questions to ask him."

She quickly explained the problem with the booking and how it had been handled. "They said that it was all arranged, but my assistant said we'd had nothing to do with it."

"Who do you believe?"

"Honestly, I'm not sure. It could have been my assistant. She is getting older. I did honor the commitment, and I came, but I didn't want to. I'm trying to avoid these talks and rallies. I'm focusing more on my books, putting my thoughts down for the wider audience. I feel I can reach more people that way." He stared at her steadily, and she shrugged. "I know you probably don't agree, but I feel like I need to do this. That it's my path." She tumbled over the words as she tried to make sense out of it all. "I just want to go home."

"And we're getting to that point," he said. "Just not yet."

She nodded and shifted. "I don't suppose you have my clothes, do you? Or can we collect it all? I really want a shower."

He looked at her in surprise and said, "You didn't bring much with you, did you?"

She shook her head. "No, I didn't. I am only here for a few days, then turn around and go home. I wasn't happy to be here so I wanted to return immediately."

"Well, I have a few things that you left in your room. You can't go back up there again."

"I don't want to," she said. "Honestly, as I said, I just want to go home."

He walked to his bag and pulled out a roll of her clothes with her paperwork.

She gasped in joy. "Oh my," she said. "I had no idea. I was so afraid my paperwork was gone, and I couldn't get home. I'd gotten into my room, unpacked some things, then went downstairs to meet a coworker but returned. They immediately attacked me at my door."

"Well, what you need to enter the country is all here," he said. And he handed everything over to her. She selected a change of clothes, got up, walked to the bathroom, and asked, "Will you be okay with him?" She stared at the prisoner malevolently. "Maybe we should hit him over the head again, just to make sure he doesn't wake up while I'm in here."

"What will you do if he does wake up?" he asked in interest.

She frowned. "I don't know," she said, "but I could help somehow. Would you knock him out again?"

"Well, if I needed to, yes," he said. "Why?"

When she didn't answer, he just smiled and said, "Go shower. I'll be fine."

"Are you sure? I don't want anything to happen to you because you came to rescue me."

"Not an issue," he said gently. "This is what I do. I'll be fine."

She hesitated but then realized that she was so damn tired, and she needed to do something fast if she hoped to accomplish anything. With a quick nod, she disappeared into the bathroom, stripped, turned on the hot shower, and finally stepped underneath the water.

Only as she stood, letting the water cascade over her head, her hands resting against the wall, supporting herself, did she let the tears flow. The occasional sob broke loose, but mostly her body heaved as the sobs rippled through her in silent motion as they always did. She wasn't a noisy crier. She was somebody who preferred the silence and to blend with it instead of disrupting it.

When she finally ran out of tears, she slowly reached for the soap and scrubbed herself down from top to bottom, then added shampoo to her hair and rinsed it out, and finally turned off the water.

She sagged to the side of the shower, tired, worn out, and shaky. But she was determined to get dressed so that she could go back outside. If she were lucky, she'd collapse on the bed for an hour or two at least. She needed a night or two to recover from this, but she didn't know how quickly she could get home, and that's where she would really recover. She was too damn grateful to be here and not wherever those horrible men had planned for her to be.

Once again dressed with her hair brushed and still wet, but too tired to use the hotel's blow-dryer, she slowly opened the door and made her way out to find Nico sitting beside one of the men who had kidnapped her. He was awake now. The kidnapper turned, looked at her, and glared. "Bitch. I told you not to make a sound."

"You did," she said with more calmness than she felt. "But why the hell should I listen to you?"

"Because now you'll die," he said simply.

She froze in place, turned to look at Nico. "Why would he say that?" she cried out in alarm.

"He's trying to scare you," Nico said. He smacked the kidnapper across his face, hard, and walked over and gave her a quick hug. "We have only the one hotel room. I can't shield you from this, so why don't you go to the bed and lie down?"

"I'm too scared to sleep," she whispered. "Yet I'm exhausted, and I need sleep, but I'm afraid that, if I do, something will happen, and he'll overpower you and take me again."

"Not gonna happen," he said, as he walked her to the bed and got her settled.

The door opened just then, and Keane walked in. He looked over at the kidnapper and smiled. "Oh, good. Time for a talk, is it?"

"Yes," Nico said. "What did you find?"

"The helicopter's gone," Keane said.

The kidnapper stared at him in shock. "No, no, it's supposed to wait for me."

"Well, guess what?" Keane said. "You missed your ride, buddy."

"That's not good," the man said. "They were very strict about making that appointment."

"Well, you don't have her to deliver to them anyway, so you're in shit for a whole lot more than just that one reason."

The guy sagged in place. "Maybe, but at least there was a hope of fixing it."

"And how do you figure that?"

"All you had to do was give her back to me, and it would be all fine."

"And why would we do that?" Nico asked in surprise.

"Because they'll still come after her. Just because I failed doesn't mean they don't still want her. They do. Now they'll just send more men."

AFTER THAT COMMENT, their prisoner shut up. Nico looked over at Keane and shrugged. "I guess he'd rather not deal with the cops and prefers to face the wrath of his coworkers."

Keane nodded. "If this is serious business, which it seems like it is, since they're killing off all the loose ends, then we have to assume that his miserable life is in danger."

"Well, I'm not protecting him," Nico said. "He's the one who screwed up. They'll take him out in their own time."

"Whether he screwed up or not, they'll take him out," Keane said. "Think about the other two."

"Right," Nico said. He returned to the bed where Charlotte lay. Her eyes were closed, and her chest rose and fell in a gentle movement. He glanced over at Keane and gave her a gentle nudge to show him that she was out.

Immediately Keane lowered his voice. "Good. That's what she needs." He went into the washroom and scrubbed down as much as he could. When he came back out, he said, "We need food, information, and to figure out how to get her home safe again."

"Good luck with that," their prisoner said in a snide voice.

"Oh, look at that. He talks," Keane said.

Their prisoner glared at them, and Nico shrugged. "I don't give a shit if they take you out or not. But any further attempts to take her out will not make us happy."

"Too late," their prisoner muttered.

"I don't understand why they even care about Charlotte," Keane said to Nico. "She's an activist, one of a thousand all around the world."

"No, she's more than that." But then the kidnapper shut his mouth tight and pinched his lips together, then glared at the two men as if sorry he had even opened his mouth.

"She's just an author who didn't even want to come to Australia. Or did you guys orchestrate that?"

The prisoner shrugged as if to say he had no clue.

That was likely the truth. *Why would anybody let a lowlife like this know any of the details?* "Oh, yeah. You weren't even part of the planning," Nico said. "You're just hired muscle. A nobody."

The prisoner continued to glare at him but didn't rise to the bait.

"Do we know anything more about the helicopter?" Nico asked Keane.

Keane sat down at the table with his laptop open. "I'm looking into it right now," he said. "I've already asked for some assistance and am tracking it down."

"I don't know about call numbers, but it should have a flight path of where it's going and where it came from."

"Doesn't mean they follow it though," Keane muttered.

Nico knew that was the truth. Even commercial planes were supposed to follow flight paths but that didn't mean they did. But, if they didn't show up on time, then inquiries were sent, and investigations were opened for missing flights. So it was to everybody's benefit to file a flight plan. Unless you didn't want anybody to know where and when you were going somewhere. In which case, better to say you didn't know. Nico was sure there were ways around doing that too.

As he sat here, studying the sleeping woman, he wondered just how far these guys would go. "I still don't understand. Why kill her? What does her death do as an activist? It turns her into a martyr, which helps her cause and not the kidnappers' cause."

"Not that these guys necessarily have the brains to think about that," Keane said. "I think you're giving them too much smarts."

Nico chuckled at that. "We never did get food."

"Order something then," Keane said, but his voice was disinterested.

Nico, on the other hand, could really use some food. He quickly put in an order through his Mavericks chat window, loving the system as it stood right now. He wasn't exactly sure who oversaw all the minions running around in the background at all these worldwide spots and whether the chat window guys were like him or if they seriously had a team admin and an espionage analyst. He liked the idea of having a whole government branch, sitting there, waiting for them to give them something to do. And then he wondered if there were more teams like his. *We need that. To better operate on a global level.*

Nico sat here wondering about that, then realized that, even if he were to ask the Mavericks, chances were nobody would say anything.

Charlotte rolled over just then. She sat up and looked at him groggily and then collapsed again.

He got up, walked over, and gently patted her shoulder, stroking her arm before picking up her hand and lacing her fingers with his. "Take it easy," he whispered, hating the deeply confused and fearful gaze that stared back at him from almost an owl-like face. He smiled, seeing that her makeup hadn't come off in the shower, and she'd been just too damn tired to even notice.

She blinked at him several more times and then whispered, "Is it safe?"

"You're still safe," he whispered. "We are still in the hotel. Four of us, including our prisoner."

At the word *prisoner*, her gaze widened. She rolled over to look at the man who had kidnapped her, still sitting at the table all tied up. She sank back down, closing her eyes and letting out a light groan. "I was hoping this was all a bad dream."

"Well, a bad dream it still could be," he said quietly, with a note of humor. "On the bright side, you were rescued and are now freshly showered and had a short nap and are in a hotel room with two guys to look after you."

The corners of her lips kicked up. "Good points," she said with a smile, speaking softly. This time her gaze was more aware and intent as she studied him. "Did you guys find out anything more?"

"Not too much, no," he whispered. "The prisoner's not talking, and we're still waiting on further information."

"Okay," she said. "How about flights back home? Did you get those booked?"

"Not sure we want to let the world know that you are flying back yet," he said, speaking softly. "At the moment you've missed your scheduled return flight. Did you consider that?"

She frowned. "No, I didn't even think of it."

"Which is a good thing, in a way," he said, whispering. "And we don't want to change that status quo, in case other people are involved in this. We need to flush them out. Otherwise you'll be looking over your shoulder for the rest of your life."

"And that's not something I want to do," she said firmly. "If I have to move to hide out, a cabin by a lake ten minutes from town would suit me fine."

"You don't worry about four-legged predators?" he asked curiously. He knew a lot of women wouldn't leave the security of town limits and their four walls where she had every available amenity at her fingertips.

But Charlotte smiled and whispered, "I like the four-legged predators. They're decent about leaving you alone, if you leave them alone. It's the two-legged ones you have to watch out for."

He agreed with her. He just found it interesting that she was of the same mind-set. "If you can go back to sleep," he said, "then I suggest you do."

She laid here with her eyes closed for a moment, but she shook her head gently and whispered, "Don't think I can." Her stomach growled just then, and she opened her eyes. "Any chance of food?"

"It's coming," he said. Just then came a knock on the door.

Immediately she cried out and huddled against the headboard.

He reached for her hands again. "It's likely food. Just stay quiet."

She stared at him, her eyes wide as she bit down on a trembling bottom lip.

"Remember. Be strong."

She took a deep breath and slowly let it out. "I think it'll take a little time for my nerves to not panic every time I hear something that surprises me."

Nico watched as Keane opened up the door to a trolley full of food. Then Nico hopped up and walked over to help his buddy. "Hope I ordered enough."

"Looks like you ordered enough for six men," Keane joked.

"One starving woman and the two of us," he said. "I'm not wasting food on the prisoner."

As Keane walked over, he caught sight of Charlotte's face. He hid his grin quickly, but not before she saw his obvious amusement.

Knowing it was the right thing to do, Nico walked back over and gave her a hand up to her feet. In a low tone, he said, "Go to the bathroom and clean your eyes. Looks like the mascara didn't come off during the shower."

She raised an eyebrow, walked into the bathroom, and let out a cry. "Oh, my word," she said. "You didn't say anything."

"I just said something now," he protested. "You were sleeping before." He could hear her running water and obviously trying to clean off her eyes, which was fine by him. With Keane's assistance, they picked up the prisoner and moved him off to the far corner. He protested, but they wouldn't have anything to do with it. "You're in the way," Nico said. "We need the table space."

"You could let me eat too," he snarled.

"Not happening," Keane said cheerfully. "Not part of my kidnapping plan." Then he gagged their prisoner. "Enough talk from you."

Nico looked up as Charlotte came out of the bathroom. Her face was clean, and she looked brighter and happier. He smiled at her and said, "Much better. Come. Sit down."

She eagerly walked toward him. "Food would be good. But a way to get home after this would be even better."

"One thing at a time," he said. He lifted the lid off the

trays of food which filled the table. To her gasp of delight, he grinned. "I have no intention of shorting you on food. So eat up. We need to be ready because we don't know what's coming."

She looked over at him and said, "It won't be a nice and simple flight home, will it?"

"No," he said, but he wouldn't say any more. Not with ears listening. He had no idea if anybody else would attack them, but what he didn't want to do was give their prisoner a tip-off as to their plans. He wasn't even sure who to turn this guy over to yet. He was waiting on that answer from his team. He figured that somebody would come and collect him soon enough. The problem was, Nico didn't want to hand him over to just anybody. It needed to be somebody helping them get Charlotte back home again. He'd rescued her, but she was a long way away from being out of danger.

They each filled up a plate and ate quietly, focused on the food.

Another knock sounded on the door. She froze, and he looked over at her, then smiled reassuringly, but he had already pulled his weapon from his holster and had her behind him. Keane raced to the door and stood behind it as Nico walked nearby and said, "Hello?"

"Let me in," came a voice from the other side.

Keane snorted. Nico stepped into the bathroom, pushing Charlotte down into the tub, and said, "Why would I do that?"

"Because you have something I want."

Immediately he cocked his handgun, still with the silencer in place, and held it up. "It's not something I'm willing to turn over."

"Well, if you don't, you'll be sorry," came the threat.

"So will you," said Nico. He looked over as Keane adjusted his stance. "If you want to talk, that's fine. Talk. Otherwise I'm not too interested in talking."

"Okay," he said. "I'll talk."

Keane silently grabbed the handle of the door. And, with Nico holding his gun at the ready, Keane suddenly opened the door. The stranger's gun came up out of nowhere, and Nico took one shot. The man standing with a handgun and a silencer fell forward with a surprised look on his face. He wasn't quite dead though, and he tried to raise his arm to fire, but Nico's second shot interrupted that thought.

Immediately Keane took a look down both ends of the hallways, then pulled the gunman into their hotel room, out of the way, and shut the door. As soon as he had him inside on the floor, they reached for towels to staunch the bleeding.

"I shot high," Nico muttered, "but he was shorter than I expected."

"You should have aimed for his eyes anyway," Keane snapped.

"Well, I figured we wouldn't get any answers that way."

With the bleeding somewhat slowed and the gunman lying on the ground, apparently unconscious, his breathing hard and raspy, Nico looked up to see Charlotte standing in front of them. "I don't even recognize him," she said. "What's he got to do with this?"

She stepped back, then turned toward the prisoner and asked, "Do you know him?" The prisoner couldn't quite see from where he was, so he shrugged.

Keane pulled out the shooter's wallet from his back pocket, but, outside of cash, there was no ID. "Hired gun?"

"I don't know what else," Nico said. "They're trying to distance themselves from this to clean up."

"So what is he? An amateur?"

"It's professional equipment though," Nico said, kicking the gun off to the side.

"And gloves. But that's almost standard."

"The real question is, did he do anything to the cameras?" Nico asked. With Keane trying to staunch the blood and to keep the guy alive, Nico walked to his laptop and quickly told his team what had happened and to arrange for a medic. And to find the camera feeds immediately for this floor. It took less than thirty seconds to get a link, and, as the link came up, there came an image of the guy's face. **Yep, that's him**, Nico said. **Track him down and follow the cameras back and see how he got in here. There could be somebody in the garage waiting for him.**

Only if he succeeded came back the answer.

True.

A name popped up. **Thomas Galloway. Walked into the underground lot on his own.**

Nico looked at his prisoner and asked him, but the prisoner shook his head. He mumbled something further.

Keane stood and took off his gag. "Repeat that."

"They said they were talking about bringing in some extra help, but I don't know that man."

There followed a simple rap sheet of breaking and entering and holding up a convenience store one night. "He's a petty thief who wants to be a bigger bad guy," Nico said, reading the doc, then he joined Keane.

"Well, whatever he was doesn't matter now," Keane said, pointing at the gunman. "He's dead."

"Of course he is. Managed an easy out for himself after all."

CHAPTER 4

CHARLOTTE DIDN'T EVEN know what to think about the men's casual attitude. But, since the gunman had come in firing, she knew there really hadn't been any other response. And she could see that any attempt to shoot reasonably high would have taken out his heart. Nico was obviously affected, although the big strong guy inside wasn't allowing him to show anything. She walked over and slipped her hand into the crook of his arm. "Well, I, for one, appreciate it."

"The question is," Keane said, alongside the dead gunman again, as he sat back on his heels and looked up at the two of them, "was he after you, Charlotte, or was he after our prisoner?"

"Oh, I never thought of that," she said. She glanced over at the prisoner. "That's possible too, isn't it?

"Particularly if they're cleaning up," Nico said, staring at his prisoner.

The guy blanched. "There's no reason for him to send a gunman after me. I already warned you that her life is in danger."

"But you didn't tell us why," Keane said.

When a series of raps came on the door, she let out a light cry and stepped behind Nico. He reached for her hand reassuringly and said, "It's okay. We know this one."

Keane opened the door, and, within seconds, the dead man was carried out. The men didn't introduce each other, and they didn't say hi. Nothing. They came in, set the gunman into a body bag, loaded him onto a body trolley—or whatever the hell that was which they used at hospitals—and took him away. Somebody else came in right behind them to clean up the blood. Not a word was spoken.

She watched in amazement at a complete industry that she had no clue even existed. When the guy was done, he left, taking all the mess with him. She looked at Keane and then whispered to Nico, "Does this always happen this way?"

Keane walked into the bathroom and washed his hands. "If you mean, do we shoot guys and have invisible teams show up and take away the body? No."

"So this is unusual then?"

"Yes," he said.

"Okay then," she said. "I wondered what crime-scene cleanup happened before the cops even got here."

"No police involvement here," Keane noted. "And we prefer not to corrupt a crime scene when they will be called in."

After a moment, when she couldn't find the right word, she said, "That was unnerving."

Nico wrapped his arms around her and walked her to the table. She kept glancing back at the door. Keane came out of the bathroom, drying his hands on a towel. She looked at him. "Are you okay?"

He tossed her a grin. "I'm fine." Then he turned to Nico and said, "We need to move."

Nico nodded and looked down at the food, but their plates were mostly empty, having had the time to eat. He glanced at her and asked, "Did you want to take any of the extra food with you?"

She looked down at the fruit and picked up an apple. "Where are we going?"

He gave her a hard smile. "Anywhere but here. Obviously we've been made."

She stopped, stared at him, and realized what he meant. "So we have to leave? And it won't be on a flight to go home, is it?"

He shook his head, but he already moved his packed bag to the front door. At an odd series of knocks on the door, he opened it and let in two other men, who quickly removed the rest of the dishes.

Nobody looked at the prisoner or made a comment about the fact that they had a man tied up or about the fresh smell of bleach either.

Nico turned to her and asked, "Do you have anything here you want to keep?"

She looked at the few bits of clothing that she had changed out of and shook her head. "Those probably need to be burned." As soon as she said that, her clothing was packed into a small bag by this newest crew and removed along with the food. The rest of the bedding was also stripped, even as Nico pushed her forward into the hallway.

"And what about him?" Charlotte asked, pointing to their tied-up prisoner. "He's being taken somewhere else too?"

One of the new guys walked up to the prisoner and smacked him hard under the jaw. When he went out cold, the new guy quickly untied him and picked him up over one shoulder, then walked him out of the room.

"This is highly illegal," she whispered in horror.

"So says you," Keane said. He nudged her forward.

"Come on. We only have two minutes with the security cameras. Let's go."

Still wrapping her mind around what was going on, she was half dragged while she half ran down to the far end of the hallway, where they ducked into the staircase and went up. As soon as they reached the fourth flight of stairs, she was getting tired, on top of already feeling shaky from what was going on. Adrenaline only carried one so far. She both wanted to run around in the same place and collapse at the same time.

"It's the adrenaline," Nico said at her side. "When it's pumping through you, it's powerful, but, when it's gone, the weakness is just as bad."

"Why are we standing on a landing in the stairwell?" she wailed. "I'd love to sit down."

"Waiting for this camera to go off."

Just then they received a beep on a phone or a watch or something. She couldn't even see what made the noise, and they didn't look to confirm, but immediately they opened the door, and she was taken to the room straight across the hallway. Once inside, they locked the door and then turned and smiled at her.

"Now you're safe again," Nico said.

"Are you sure?"

He nodded. "Sit down and eat your apple."

She stared at the apple in her hand, took a big bite, more because she needed something to stop her jaw from clenching than anything. She collapsed on the bed closest to her and said, "What was that all about?"

"Obviously somebody knew where we were and where the prisoner was," Keane said coolly. "We had to make sure that, if our prisoner or our gunman or his driver had had time to get a message out, nobody would find us before we changed locations again."

"Shouldn't we get out of this hotel then?" She glanced around at the walls closing in on her. "Surely it's not safe to be here at all."

Nico smiled and nodded. "We're making that happen too."

"Good," she said. "An airline right back home again works for me, by the way."

"Well, it won't work so well for us," he said. "Again we don't want your face on any of the customs and immigration points of entry."

"Why not?"

"So nobody knows where you are," Nico said. "The best thing for you is to just rest."

"A little hard to do," she said. "My nerves are on edge."

"Well, there's a minibar," Keane said helpfully. "How about a shot of whiskey?"

"How about coffee?" she shot back. "I didn't get to have mine."

"We can get you some room service again," Nico said cheerfully. "But I highly doubt caffeine will help with the nerves."

"I'm not sure I care at this point," she said. "Coffee's a comfort as much as anything." Then she got more comfortable on the bed and wondered about what exactly just happened. What really blew her away was the efficiency with which things happened. "So, if you can make all this happen—dead bodies disappear, et cetera," she said, "you do have a plan to get me home, right?"

"Right," Nico said. "It'll be a little unorthodox though."

"I don't care how orthodox it is," she said. "I still have

my passport, so I can get into the country from any point of entry."

"Exactly," he said. "So it might surprise you which point we end up choosing." But he refused to say any more.

That bothered her too, but she couldn't do a whole lot about it. She found herself shivering as she laid here on the bed.

Nico made a grunt and came over and picked up a blanket from the other bed, then tossed it over her. "It *was* adrenaline. Now that's shock," he said. "Curl up. Know that you're safe and that we've got this."

And, for the first time, she started to believe it. "I'd do a lot to avoid being recaptured again," she whispered.

He ever-so-gently stroked her cheek and whispered back, "I have no intention of losing you again."

She closed her eyes and huddled under the blanket, her body slowly calming down. She didn't even want to dwell on the crime-scene cleanup, but it was hard not to when she saw just how efficient and smooth the other people's actions had been. She couldn't imagine what all these guys were trying to do and how much effort they had gone through to do it.

A whole team had come in and swept out the place, then cleaned it up and swiped it of fingerprints and that body. ... Sure, a service elevator was here, and it wasn't even that far away, but somebody had shut down the cameras to let them all escape detection. The same thing had been done to the cameras that had enabled her kidnappers to get her out of the original hotel room and to move her out too. "Who was that who took off with the prisoner?"

"A government agency rep."

"Do you think our prisoner was connected with some government plot?" she asked, bewildered.

"Not necessarily," Nico said. "We have to consider all avenues."

"Like what?"

"Like your family," Keane said suddenly.

She looked at him in surprise, but Nico's phone buzzed, gathering her attention now.

He looked up to read the text and walked to the front door. "Coffee's here." He opened the door and pulled in a cart.

And she realized that the text had told him that it was outside the door. She shook her head. "So now they won't knock?"

He grinned at her. "Here," he said and pushed the trolley between the two beds.

She looked to see a beautiful latte with a pattern on the top. She smiled. "So, even in times of stress like this, I get something pretty."

"Is there a reason not to enjoy every moment?"

"I think I have even more reason to enjoy every moment," she said.

"Especially now."

She sat up, lifted the cup, and took a sip. Then she put it on the night table and hitched her butt backward, so she could lean against the headboard with the blanket up around her chest and then hugged her coffee again.

He returned to the silver coffee carafe. He poured two cups, for him and Keane.

"How did you guys know I like lattes?"

"We know everything," Keane said in a dry tone.

She winced at that. "Well, I hope not," she said.

"And why is that?" Nico asked.

"Nobody wants their entire life completely opened for

viewing."

"Very few people ever get to see the details," Nico said. He again turned toward the trolley and lifted the lid off the dome in the center.

She'd seen it there but hadn't even registered it—or what was under it. A big plate of cookies and muffins. She cried out in delight and immediately snatched a muffin.

He stared at her. "Are you still hungry?"

"Well, I ate the apple to give my jaw something to work on," she said by way of explanation. "But this looked so good. And I guess maybe I am a little hungry."

Nico offered Keane something off the plate, and, when the plate was returned to the trolley, she still saw several cookies and another muffin. She had no intention of being ladylike and not indulging. She was still hungry and still afraid that whatever was coming would be a little harder than anything she'd seen yet. "Are you going to tell me any details about how we're leaving?"

"No," Nico said, "not yet."

"Right," she said. "I'll just sit here and eat then."

"You do that," he said.

And she did, but, after the coffee and the food, she felt sleepy again. "You guys won't leave me alone, right?"

Nico looked over with a smile and said, "Go to sleep. I'll wake you when we're ready to leave."

She stared at him in surprise. "Are we leaving tonight? Well, I guess it's technically morning."

"In a few hours," he said. "Go ahead and sleep. It's the best answer yet."

Not being able to get any more information out of him, she curled up and laid her head on the pillow, then pulled the blanket back up to her chin and fell asleep.

"YOU'RE GETTING TOO attached," Keane growled.

"I don't think so," Nico said. "I'm just a little friendlier than you are."

"It seems to me that you're getting too attached."

Nico ignored Keane. Nico's partner was big and gruff, but he had the heart of a teddy bear. They were just trying to make this as easy on Charlotte as possible. Nico got up and moved the trolley out of the way, so, if she had to get up in the night when she was still groggy, she wouldn't trip over it. She'd left them two cookies, one each. He handed one to Keane and then took the last one, collecting all the dishes as he put the trolley back outside the door. "Do we have an update on the timeline?"

"Helicopter's arriving on the roof in one hour and forty."

"It's not quite enough sleep for her, but anything she gets is good."

"It'll be all she gets for a little while," Keane noted.

Nico nodded. "It should be an interesting trip."

"Well, it's the way this has panned out," Keane said. "We have a long way to go to get back. The flight's the most direct, but, short of a private jet on a private airstrip, it won't be the easiest way to go."

"That's all right," Nico said. "I'm okay to go back on a cruiser or a submarine or whatever."

"It'll be a combination," he said with a smile.

"Right." Nico sat down and worked on his research. "I'd like answers from that damn idiot though."

"Not to mention the shooter."

"All that the Mavericks team says on the shooter is how

he was carrying a wad of cash, and they suspect he was paid for the job."

"Which we already figured out," Keane said in a dry tone. "So that's really not helpful."

"I know," he said. "So we focus on the last two men of the kidnapping team. The one we caught and the one we haven't seen yet."

"And whether the shooter was the mastermind or if he's just another minion."

"I'd say minion."

"She didn't recognize him though."

Nico nodded. "Still, you'd think getting more men involved would make it even messier. Or they suspected that, if the shooter failed, we'd have killed him anyway."

Just then the chat window opened up, and a picture of a fourth male came up. **A search of the local reports by Australian authorities regarding gunshot wounds tracked the gun used to kill the first two DBs.**

"Good. Now if only we can find the fourth man," Nico said, sharing this newest intel with Keane. "Still our bloody prisoner should be damn glad he's alive."

"Interesting," Keane said. "So they're cleaning up and getting rid of everybody."

"Which means they're changing the operation or moving it."

"I'd say more like shutting it down," Keane said quietly. "We've got her, and it's obvious we won't give her up."

"Or they'll lie low and grab her later."

"We're thinking it's about the brother?"

Yes," Nico said. "At the mention of her family earlier, she looked more puzzled than anything."

A soft voice spoke from the bed. "That's because I don't

have any family," she said. "I don't know what you're talking about. Your records surely would show that I was in foster care."

"You had a brother," Keane said. "What happened to him?"

"I don't know," she said. "We were separated when I was in fourth grade, and he was in second. I never saw him again. I've tried contacting the adoption agencies and foster care, but nobody will give me any information."

"And yet they didn't tell you that he had passed on or anything else?"

She shook her head. "No, nobody will tell me anything."

The two men exchanged hard glances.

She sat up slowly. "What do you know that I don't know?"

Nico drummed his fingers on the table, waiting to see what Keane would say.

Keane looked at Nico and said, "It might have something to do with him."

"What might?" she asked.

"This kidnapping," Nico said.

"Only if he's alive and if he's some prominent businessman that I don't know about," she said. "Otherwise who'd care?"

"Nobody said anything to you at all, huh?" Keane asked.

"I told you," she said, as she stifled a yawn. "Nobody told me anything."

Keane asked, "And you just automatically put down your kidnapping to your activism?"

She shrugged. "It makes sense. I pissed off a lot of people. But all this killing? … None of that makes any sense."

That part bothered Nico too. "Did anyone attack any of

the rallies you've attended, bring weapons of any kind? Bombs? Something more organized?"

She stared at him in surprise. "No. Nothing."

"Any of the organizers being blackmailed? Threatened in any way?"

"Not that I know of." She shook her head. "Maybe you guys should be the ones to answer that question."

"We're looking into it, but a lot of people were here for this Australian rally."

"Check the organizers because, like I said, they didn't have any reason for me to come over here. But I ended up giving in anyway."

"Was that you giving in or your assistant forcing you to give in?"

"Well, Maggie's very good at coercion," she admitted with a wince. "She doesn't travel with me, but she was adamant that I came."

"What's her name?" Nico asked, hearing Charlotte's response and typing in the name of her assistant. "Maybe this has something to do with her."

"I doubt it. She's like sixty-five years old and has nothing to do with anything. She's only worked for me for six months, but she's a godsend."

At that, the two men exchanged glances and bent down to their laptops.

Her soft voice drifted toward Nico. "You can dig as much as you want," she said, "but I'm telling you that you won't find anything."

"Why is that?"

"Because she's the sweetest, nicest person I've ever met," she said. "She's the mother I never had."

"What happened to your parents?"

"They died in a car accident."

"And your brother?"

"I don't know," she said. "When you're in foster care, you're surviving day to day. I was traumatized when they split me and my brother up, and it's always been in the back of my mind that he's out there somewhere. But I didn't know for sure that he is. It's a sucky system where they don't let you find your other family members."

"I thought they did?"

"Then other people know what buttons to push that I don't," she snapped. "I couldn't get any information out of anybody."

"We might be able to take a look," Keane said.

At that, Nico raised an eyebrow. It wasn't for them to say anything without getting some actual word, but he could understand her wanting to know something about her family.

"Well, if you have any more pull than I do," she said in surprise, "I'd really appreciate it."

Nico kept his thoughts to himself, but just because Maggie was a nice old lady didn't make a damn bit of difference in his world. He would like to see Charlotte reconnect with her brother, particularly if there wasn't any reason not to. He quickly sent a message to his team. **Find the brother. I think it's time Charlotte got reacquainted.**

The message came back with a question mark, meaning, they didn't know but they'd make inquiries. **Is it related?**

No clue yet. Check on her assistant right now.

Name?

He typed it in and said, **She hasn't worked there very long.**

Nico then glanced at Charlotte. "How long have you known Maggie?"

CHAPTER 5

CHARLOTTE SHRUGGED. "SHE was always there in the periphery of my world for the last couple years. I used to see her often, sit down, and have a cup of tea with her. Only when I needed an assistant, after my other assistant left, then I considered hiring Maggie. She was in a tough spot, down on her luck, and just needed to have something, even part-time."

"What happened to your previous assistant?" Keane asked.

"From one day to the next, she disappeared," Charlotte said in a harsh tone. "I contacted the police when she didn't show up and filed a missing person's report, but I never heard anything more."

Nico sat back at that news. "That's another major issue to have come up in your life in the last year then, isn't that?"

"Well, sure," she said, "but it's not *my* issue. It's not my world. I mean, obviously it was tough losing her. But I mean—" Then she stopped, her voice faltering. "Let me put it this way. I wasn't terribly friendly with her. She was doing a job for me, but she wasn't doing it the best that she could. I wasn't sure how to fire her because I had nobody to replace her. She was barely doing what I needed done, so I was almost ambivalent.

"As it was, she didn't show up for work one day, and I

assumed she'd gotten another job. I had her new phone number, but she never answered. I did drive by her place and knocked on her door, and no one was there. Honestly, I figured she just had had enough of me and buggered off. She was always talking about going back East anyway."

"Is that the working mentality of the youth these days?" Keane asked, his lips quirking.

"I don't know what it is," she said. "It was frustrating at the time mostly because, if she had just told me, it would have been fine. But to not show up from one day to the next, what was I supposed to think?"

"Did she have a boyfriend?"

"Yes, and, when I knocked on her neighbor's apartment, they basically shrugged and said that they hadn't seen her in weeks anyway."

"Meaning that she was staying all the time with her boy-friend?"

"I think so, yes. I haven't seen her since. I don't know if she sees me and avoids me or if it's just the fact that our paths don't cross, and that's the way she likes it."

"Interesting. Did you pay her fully?"

"I paid her up to the last day as per our agreement," she said with a nod. "But I deposited the money into her account."

"Do you have her account info?"

She looked at him in surprise and then sat up slowly and said, "Well, I'm sure I can find it. But I don't have my phone."

"And there was no laptop in your room, was there?"

She shrugged. "No, I forgot it at home. I could use one of your laptops to log on to my account though."

"We found no purse either. Do the kidnappers have it?"

Charlotte shook her head. "No. I don't carry a purse usually. Not at home and not when traveling for sure."

"So, did you always transfer funds for your previous assistant's wages?"

"Sometimes I transferred, and sometimes I walked over and deposited a check."

Keane stepped aside and said, "Here. You can use my laptop if you like."

She walked over and sat down, then brought up a new page, logged into her bank account, and searched back by date. "Here it is," she said. "I always put it in my notes when I do a transfer like this."

He quickly read off the account number to Nico.

And, with that, she logged off and stepped away from the laptop. She walked to the window and stared out into the odd light outside. "It feels so surreal," she murmured.

"Yeah, when you get into a scenario like this, it certainly leads you away from the mom-and-pop type of living that you were doing."

"And I already lived a little bit on the left-wing," she murmured. "I was trying to get out of all this. But …"

"When was the last time you attended a rally like that?"

"Two years ago in England," she said. "That was just a little too violent for me too."

"Did something happen there?" Nico asked, his voice sharp.

She turned to look at him and gave him a soft smile, then shook her head. "No, I was just thinking that all the rallies did were incite the people to get hotter about the issues. Change wasn't really happening, and, if my job was to get the word out, then I had a better chance of doing that through my books."

"Maybe," he said in a noncommittal tone. "It does make you a little less visible on a personal level than speaking at rallies."

"That was another consideration," she said. She leaned against the window ledge and just looked at the city lights twinkling all around them. It was gorgeous, but, at the same time, she now knew that an underbelly of evil and nastiness she couldn't even begin to contemplate was out there too. "Do you think the prisoner will be okay?"

"Not likely," Keane said, not holding any punches. "If he's visible and available, the mastermind behind this kidnapping will probably take him out. Otherwise he'll be locked up for his crimes."

"And the kidnapping? That's only if I press charges, isn't it?"

"And are you telling me that you wouldn't?" Nico stared at her in astonishment.

She frowned at him. "I don't really want to be part of a trial on another spectacle like that."

"*Another* spectacle?"

"You know what I mean," she said irritably. "They'd make a case like mine blow up, and it would be a zoo. Honestly, I'm pretty well done with being a physical public figure."

Just then another buzz went off. She glanced at them. "You guys make more noise ..."

"No," he said, "not anymore."

She watched as they quickly packed up. And then she realized they were leaving. "Now?"

He nodded. "Now."

With his bag collected, he reached out a hand, and instinctively she placed hers in it.

"This is becoming a habit," she joked.

"Which part's a habit? Holding hands or moving from place to place under the cover of darkness?"

"Both," she said. "I don't mind the first, but the second one sucks."

At that, Keane gave a peal of shallow laughter. "He's single and available, so you can keep doing the hand-holding thing."

She rolled her eyes at him. They were already outside and in the hallway. But, once they got to the stairs, they climbed and climbed and climbed. She took several deep breaths at one of the landings and asked, "How much farther?"

"Just a few more," Nico said patiently as he stood two steps above, waiting for her.

"Are we going to the roof or something?"

"Or something," he said with a nod.

She stared at him in surprise, then gave a head shake and quickly gathered up her energy and followed. When they came to the door at the very top and entered onto the roof, she laughed. "You weren't kidding." But then she saw the helicopter, sitting there, waiting for them. It was off, and the rotors were still. "Is there a pilot for that thing?"

"Yeah," Nico said. "Me." They walked over, and he quickly helped her up into the side, then looked over at Keane. "Might need you up front."

"Yeah," Keane said.

Nico hopped into the front, put on his headset, and started up the engine. "What I don't have is any navigational markers for where we're going," Nico said.

She leaned forward from the back seat. "Are you saying that you don't know where we're flying to?"

"Oh, I know where we're flying to," he said. "The trouble is, our destination's on the move too."

And, with that, he laughed and slowly navigated the helicopter into the night.

NICO WAS NEVER happier than when he was flying, unless maybe when on a big ship. He was definitely an air and sea boy, and it didn't matter to him which. He'd picked up his helicopter license when he was quite young, and it had come in handy through all his navy training as well. His years as a SEAL meant that he, even though not scheduled as a pilot for a lot of the missions, was a pinch hitter when needed. He had stepped in and taken some of these birds home after pilots were shot or injured. In other words, Nico did what needed to be done, many times over. But now, flying over the ocean, it was special. He smiled and looked at the scenery all around him, then said, "You almost forget."

"Almost," Keane said. He was busy contacting their landing position. "I have it up here. You're heading forward another twenty-seven nautical miles, and we're going due east another twelve degrees."

He quickly made his adjustments. "And they're expecting us?"

"They are."

Nico nodded. "That's good. This bird will fly for a while, but we'll have to fuel up somewhere."

"Our destination is out in international waters right now, and she's a little bit farther ahead, so we'll probably take about an hour to get there."

"Good enough." He tapped his comm on his headset

and called back to Charlotte. "We have about an hour of flight time," he said. "Sit back, relax, and enjoy."

"Will do," she said. Then she added, "You're a man of amazing mystery."

"I'm just a man," he said. "Nothing more, nothing less."

She didn't answer that, but he could see that she was settled in and staring out at the ocean below.

"I always find that I fall asleep if I'm sitting and looking at the water," Keane said.

"It's pretty special," Nico said with a nod. "There's just something about the endless waves on the horizon."

But he could see up ahead the lights of where he was going.

They landed four minutes early, coming down on the huge USS *Bainbridge*. It brought back so many memories for Nico, and it felt almost like coming home. By the time he shut off his rotors, hopped out, and walked around to open up the passenger side and to assist Charlotte onto the deck, he was as comfortable here as he had been up there.

She looked around at the completely different scenario and stared at him. "Are we on a warship?"

"Well, we're on one of America's ships, compliments of the US Navy, yes," he said. "But we're hardly at war."

"I didn't really mean that we're at war."

He nodded. "I know what you meant. And, yes, this is the USS *Bainbridge*."

She nodded and smiled. "Am I allowed to be here?"

"Well, not very many people will know you're here," he said. And with his bag and once again holding her hand gently, he led her toward one seaman, standing but not looking at them, yet he saluted nonetheless as Nico and his party went past. Nico nodded to the sailor and kept on going.

"Have you ever been on this one before?" she asked.

"I have," he said cheerfully. He led her down to the cabin area, marked off the one that they'd been assigned, quickly opened it, and pointed her inside. "Up or down bunk?"

She looked to see four bunks and shrugged. "I'll take an upper bunk."

"Done," he said. He picked her up and gently popped her onto the top bunk.

She let out half a shriek and said, "That's it? We're just here now?"

"That's it," he said. "Now sleep. It's been a rough night."

"You're not kidding." She rolled over and faced the wall. "You'll wake me if anything happens, right?"

"Hasn't enough happened yet?"

She chuckled. "Absolutely. I'm just too damn tired now to watch and wait and see for myself."

And, with that, she fell into a deep sleep. He dropped his bag at the end of the bunk below her. With Keane crashing on the opposite bunk, he stepped out to see if anybody was around. Instead he found an envelope on the floor outside his door. He picked it up and stepped back inside.

"What have we got?" Keane asked.

"Instructions apparently," he said. "Sitting there and waiting outside."

"It always blows me away that you can be on a ship so full of men, and yet nobody sees anything."

"It's what the military is good for, following orders," Nico muttered. He walked over to the far end, where a tiny table was, and sat down. He brought out everything and took a look. "Interesting," he said. "Included a photo of her assistant in here."

"And why is that?"

"Because she's dead."

Immediately Keane hopped off his bunk and came over. "The previous assistant or the new assistant?"

"The previous one," Nico said, his voice dark. He held up the image and said, "She can't be twenty-seven or -eight."

Keane looked at it and nodded. "And do we know how she died?"

"Hit-and-run apparently. She never had a chance, mowed down while she was walking home one evening."

"I wonder if it's connected."

Nico tossed a glance at Charlotte. "I don't see how it can't be."

"Ditto. More coincidences than I'm prepared to accept at this point." Keane sat down and tugged some of the other papers toward him. Together, they went through every bit of information they'd been given, but there wasn't a whole lot. Mostly just their travel plans. "This should be fun," he said.

"Yeah. But at least part of the journey will be on a private jet."

"I'm all for that too," he said. "I wasn't really thinking that we would make it home that fast, but this way we'll be there soon."

"And I'm thinking that's a good thing for her to disappear from sight even when we get her home—at least until this is over."

"Unless they're waiting for her to show up back home again."

"That's my concern," Nico said. He opened up his laptop and sent off a message, making sure that undercover security would be at her house before they arrived and continuing until the kidnapping mastermind was caught. As an afterthought, he added, **Make sure you sweep for bugs.**

Will check came the response.

"And why would the previous assistant be killed, even if her death is connected? Other than tying up loose ends. We still don't know why Charlotte is even involved," Keane said thoughtfully.

"I don't know," Nico said in bewilderment. "None of it makes any sense."

"And unfortunately what we do know," Keane said, "is that, as soon as it does make sense, we'll be in crunch time."

"Yeah. We never really find out the actual details until we get to the end of this shit, do we?"

"No, it's usually a FUBAR session when everybody finds out what's going on."

"It'd be nice to change that for once," Nico said. "We could maybe get answers before everyone is in danger."

"Yeah? Let me know how that works out for you," Keane said.

CHAPTER 6

W HEN CHARLOTTE WOKE up the next morning, her bladder screamed at her. She rolled over to see the room was lit, if it could even be considered a room. It was small and sparse of furniture, very military, with double bunks on both sides and a very small table at the far end. There was a little bit more, but nothing that really caught her eye as her bladder screamed for release. She slowly slid down over the edge of her upper bunk and stepped onto the cold floor. She gasped, and instantly Nico sat up on the bunker below hers. "Are you okay?"

"Yes, but I need the washroom."

He led her to the bathroom and said, "We have our own."

Grateful, she walked in and closed the small door. It was almost as small as an airline bathroom. A little bit bigger but still it was a bathroom. And when she used the facilities and stood and washed her hands, she was beyond relieved. She checked her face, but she looked pretty decent, considering her kidnapping and all. Although she was still tired from the night's goings-on, she had had some rest. As she opened the door, Nico leaned against the wall. She got out of his way so he could use it behind her. And then she returned to the bunks.

Keane lay on the other lower bunk with his eyes closed.

She didn't know if he was asleep or awake. She sat down on the lower bunk that Nico had vacated and waited until he came back. When he saw her sitting there, he stretched out and patted the bed beside her. "At least this way we can talk," he murmured.

Not wanting to wake Keane, she stretched out beside Nico and whispered, "How long are we here for?"

"Quite a while," he said. "But we're on the move, and we're heading off to a new destination. We've got several different legs to this journey, but they will get us home again."

"Sounds good to me," she said with a yawn.

He whispered, "Can you sleep some more?"

"I don't think so," she murmured, but she could already feel the drowsiness coming over her. "Or maybe I can." She curled her knees up to her chest and whispered, "I should have gone to my bunk."

"No need. Just rest."

Her eyes already closed, she smiled. "What about you though?"

"I'm a big boy," he said. "Besides, I have work to do."

She heard him, but that's about all she heard. She nodded. "Make sure you wake me if anything happens." She knew it was becoming a habit to ask that of him. She just didn't know why it was so important.

"Just forget about everything, and go back to sleep."

NICO WATCHED AS she drifted back to sleep again; then he slowly sat up and shifted around her.

Keane opened his eyes and looked over with a smile.

"Just like a homing pigeon."

"Ha," Nico said. "I'll check our time schedule."

"We've still got six more hours."

Just then there was a beep. Nico checked the chat box to see transportation changes. He softly called over to Keane. "They've changed our plan. The private jet is no longer in the mix."

"I wonder why."

"No way to know," he said. "But one of the stations, Thailand, is sending a military plane back home again."

"And we're going on it?"

"Looks like it. They're heading to Alaska first."

"And then what? We're switching?"

Nico nodded. "Yes."

"What time frame?"

"Two hours."

"That's enough for her to get some more sleep. Cargo planes won't be an easy way to rest."

"Nope, definitely not. But that's all right. She can sit buckled in, and, in time, we'll get where we need to."

"I wonder why Alaska."

"Well, we're way the hell on the other side of the world, so why not? We have to go one direction or the other."

"I was hoping for a jaunt into Germany," Keane said with a half a smile. "Not that we'd get off the base at any time."

"I was just hoping for a direct from Sydney to San Fran myself," Nico said, a grin splitting his face.

"It's never that easy," Keane said with a laugh.

"No, it never is."

Nico woke Charlotte fifteen minutes before they were due to leave. When she stared at him with bleary eyes, he smiled and said, "Go wash your face. We'll leave here soon."

She nodded and got ready.

With his bag in hand, he grabbed her hand and said, "Don't say a word as we leave, please."

Again she nodded, and he went ahead. She followed, with Keane bringing up the rear. Back up on deck, she was led to a different helicopter. Only this time Nico wasn't flying. She raised her eyebrows at him as he sat down beside her. He shook his head and said, "He's bringing the helicopter back."

She nodded in understanding and watched as they took off, staring down at the massive ship below them. "I wish I'd gotten a tour."

"Not happening," he said. "As in never happening."

"Too bad," she said. "That was an experience of a lifetime."

"And hopefully the only time you have to hide out on a carrier like that," he said with half a chuckle.

She smiled. "So, where will we go next?"

He winked at her. "Wait and see."

CHAPTER 7

W HEN THEY LANDED at a military base, Charlotte smiled and said, "So I guess I get a military escort home?"

"Not quite," Nico said. "It won't be anywhere near as comfortable."

She groaned. "So, no royal treatment for me?"

"No," he said. "We're doing this on the side. Nobody here knows who you are or what you are."

"Good. Anonymity is a great idea, especially right now." When she was escorted off the helicopter, she turned to thank the pilot, but Nico nudged her forward. "It's just good manners," she said. She'd been given a little bit of warning, but she hadn't expected these conditions. She almost laughed when she walked up to the plane with the two men at her side. Several other military personnel headed onto the same airplane, but it was much less of an airliner and definitely didn't come with stewardesses or meals or any of the other comforts that she was accustomed to.

It did, however, come with pallets of cargo strapped on tight to the floor and seats at the sides that appeared to be mostly boards, harder and more unyielding than she had ever thought possible. Alongside her was a harness strap that kept her in place, which was a good thing as she soon learned. But her ride didn't provide earplugs, and she could use those too.

Nico leaned closer and whispered, "If you can sleep, do so."

She quirked her lips at him. "Meaning that there's not much else to do?"

He nodded. "You'll find everybody zoning in and out."

"It's awfully noisy," she murmured.

"It's a cargo plane that carries personnel," he said.

"And we have a long way to go, right?"

"We do," he said with a laugh. "But we'll get there pretty fast, all things considered."

She nodded and closed her eyes, but, instead of sleeping, she tried to meditate and to let the stress of the last two days slide off her back. She hated the fact that these men were looking at her assistant Maggie. But Charlotte had heard them earlier, talking about Vanessa, how she'd been found after a hit-and-run. Charlotte couldn't even believe that the poor young woman was dead.

It never occurred to Charlotte that something like that might have happened. Well, it had occurred to her but not seriously. She'd been sure that Vanessa had taken off with her boyfriend. Charlotte had figured that the job was something Vanessa didn't want to do anymore. But, to find out that she was dead, and Charlotte hadn't even known, and that she'd had such negative thoughts about a poor woman who couldn't even defend herself made Charlotte feel like a heel. "Did they ever find out who killed my assistant?"

Nico's head pivoted suddenly in her direction. "You heard us?"

She nodded. "Was the hit-and-run driver ever caught?"

"Not according to her file."

She nodded sadly. "She was such a young woman. She

didn't deserve that."

"I'm pretty sure nobody in this world deserves to be mowed down on a sidewalk like that."

"Your terminology?" She rolled her head toward him and looked at him. "Was it deliberate?" He didn't answer, but she saw it in his eyes anyway. She slowly straightened and looked around. Everybody else had their eyes closed or talked among themselves. She hissed, "Seriously?"

He shrugged. "We don't have answers yet," he reminded her gently.

"Why not?" she cried out in a soft voice like a child. "We need answers."

"And we're getting a lot of them," he said.

She nodded and collapsed back, her head leaning against the wall. "But that's just terrible. I don't understand why these people would directly target me or those around me."

"No," Nico said, "but there'll be a reason. There's always a reason, whether we see it at first or not. The worst is when we never uncover a motive. Then it eats at us forever."

"I don't want there to be a reason," she said, hating the petulance in her voice.

NICO WANTED TO ask her a lot of questions but not in a scenario where anybody could overhear. The best thing to do was just put in their time. And it seemed like forever when he finally got word that they would be disembarking. He looked down to see she was still asleep, her head against his shoulder and her arms curled up into her chest as she tried to shift sideways. She would be damn sore and stiff after this ordeal, but at least they were landing on American soil again.

He nudged her gently and whispered in her ear, "Hey, wake up. We're coming in for a landing."

She opened her eyes and blinked at him and then widened her eyes as she stared around, reality slamming back into her. She nodded and said, "Good. These seats are horrible."

He grinned at her. "But the price is right."

She laughed. "I doubt the airline'll refund the flight I missed though," she said.

"No, I don't imagine they will. But maybe because it was a kidnapping, they might."

"We'll see," she said. "I'll have to take it up with them when I get back home again."

He helped her disembark, and, as they stood at the base, she asked, "Now what?"

"Now," he said, "we're leaving again."

And he walked her across to a different pad where another plane was waiting. She groaned. "Another one?"

"Another one," he said.

"Well, thank you for getting me home."

"Getting you home without everybody in the world knowing."

She winced at that. "I didn't think about the media hype. I'm sure they all heard I was kidnapped, so they'd be all over the place every step of the way."

"Goes along with being a public figure," Keane said cheerfully.

"I don't want to be a public figure," she said. "Remember that part about staying home and writing books?"

"A lot of authors are public figures too," Keane said. "Did you consider that?"

"I wasn't planning on doing anything that would be

quite so popular. I more or less needed to convey the words in my mind that need to be spoken in a much less volatile way."

Keane laughed at that. "I suspect you're the kind of person who causes chaos no matter where she goes." He turned to look at Nico and said, "You better keep that in mind."

She glared at him. "That's not funny."

He laughed and said, "Absolutely it is."

Inside the next plane, she realized it was the same damn thing again. Nico buckled her down, and it took another forty minutes before they were airborne again. "So now, what do we do on this flight? I'm too achy to sleep more."

He shrugged and said, "What do you want to talk about then?"

"Something that doesn't involve this case."

"So tell me about your childhood."

"It was glorious, and then my parents died. And that's the end."

"And you don't remember the details?"

She shook her head. "I don't think I want to remember the details. I was first in foster care for all of grade four, I believe. Even the details get hazy though. Most of the time I hated so many of the foster homes."

"Were your foster parents so bad?" Keane asked on the other side of her.

"No, I just think they were so busy with a lot of kids that they couldn't deal with one who was too traumatized. I wasn't an easy child during that time."

They nodded. "Did they say why you and your brother were split up?"

"That's easy," she said. "He was much more difficult to handle. He was really angry, threw lots of fits, was hard to control. He was removed from the home and went to another place."

"Well, hopefully at the other place, he got some help for the anger and the grief that had to have been choking him."

"Maybe," she said, "but I don't know about that. I didn't get a chance to find out because I never saw him again. And that ended up making me feel even angrier."

"What about your marriage?" Nico asked.

She shut up on that topic.

Now that was an interesting reaction. He leaned over and studied her face. "What aren't you telling me?"

She shrugged. "Just more guilt," she snapped. "Do we really have to talk about that?"

He didn't know what to say because *guilt* wasn't what he expected.

"Why would you feel guilty?" he asked. "I gather you weren't happily married?"

"I was very happily married," she murmured, dropping her head back and closing her eyes again, rather than seeing their faces. "My husband got sick right away, probably had been sick before I met him and before we got married. His treatments were difficult, and his medications were even worse, and he changed. And, no, it wasn't his fault. And, no, I didn't love him any less. But living with him was not easy."

"What medications?"

"He had brain cancer and a couple other sideline issues that just seemed to make life even more difficult. But he kept reacting to the medications. He would get angry. He gained fifty, sixty, seventy pounds, and his face would blow up and swell, and he'd have trouble going to the bathroom. It was really hard on him."

"Sounds like it was hard on you too."

"But nobody ever thinks about that," she said. "You're supposed to be there for your spouse, for the person you love. You nurse them through sickness and health, but nobody tells you that, from the time you've come home from your honeymoon, it's possible to get so badly sick." She swallowed, then whispered, "It was a brain tumor, and it took him five years to die. Five years where I watched the beautiful future I had hoped for and the man I loved go through endless pain and torment. At the same time, every time his medication was changed, he would go through this personality shift and …" She fell silent. "Listen to me. I'm bitching about how he acted, and yet he's the one who died."

"I think part of the problem," Nico said quietly, "is you feel guilty because you felt the way that you felt."

"Sure," she said. "Wouldn't you?"

"Well, I would hope that I'd understand that that's where I needed to be and that I did the best I could and then move on."

"Well, the trouble is, I haven't moved on," she snapped. "I still feel guilty for not being the perfect angelic wife that I was supposed to be."

"Did you yell at him?" Nico asked. "Did you tell him off for being who he was? Did you get angry that he was sick? Did you let him see it?"

She stared at Nico in horror. "Of course not. I'd never do that. He was the one who was already going through all the trauma. I wouldn't add to it."

"Exactly," he said. "So why do you feel guilty? You're human. You were taken to the edge of your endurance. You had to watch somebody you love die in a slow and painful way. I hardly think that's something you should feel guilty about."

She frowned at him. "So how come it sounds completely normal when you say it, but it's hard for me to clear my head from anything other than feeling bad because I could have done better?"

"Think back to the days that you looked after him. Some of the worst days of your life. How exhausted you were, getting up at nighttime, how exhausted you were during the day because it never ended. Do you really think you could have done more?"

"No," she whispered, tears in the corners of her eyes. She brushed them away impatiently. "There were days where I went and cried in the shower. Sometimes two in one day just so I could bawl and not have him know. It was torture."

"I think a lot of that is survivor's guilt," he said softly. "And I do understand that too."

"And how is that?"

"Because I worked as a SEAL before this. I've been there where my buddies all died in missions, and I survived. You don't want to be the only person who walks away, where everybody looks at you and wonders why you lived and why not the guys with the families and the kids and parents they supported, instead of the single guy who appeared to have nothing and nobody waiting for him and not even a scratch on his body."

She opened her eyes. "Wow," she said. "I imagine that's pretty tough."

"It is tough," Nico said. "But I had no explanation for why I survived, and the others didn't either, except they would say it wasn't my time. For me, it was like, why not my time? Why would I survive, and they didn't?" he murmured. "But your only choice is to deal with the circumstances, and then you move on."

"So maybe I haven't moved on," she whispered.

"You haven't," he said. "But this is a really good time to let it all go. And maybe you won't have quite so much anger in your world, and you can find peace inside for when you write your books."

He settled back and closed his eyes, leaving her to her thoughts. It was his own accident in his mind that he kept dealing with over and over again. He knew his own words needed to be taken to heart himself, but it was hard sometimes. Survivor's guilt was something he wouldn't wish on anybody.

CHAPTER 8

L ANDING THE NEXT time at the Coronado base in California was the end to a long, arduous journey. And Charlotte was never more grateful to get home than she was then. She stretched her arms up and around, loving the heat, loving the noise, loving the smog and everything about it.

"I do love California," she said, crying out in joy.

"Good," he said. "The day's about to start, at least for us. For this town, it's already after lunch. Let's see if we can get you home."

"Sounds good to me," she said. "It might be afternoon, but I'm more than done."

"That last trip wasn't too bad, was it?"

"It was all rough," she said. "My butt's killing me. I don't think I want to sit for a week."

"Well, you have to sit in the vehicle," Keane said. As they walked out onto the base, he signed off for a vehicle and hopped into an army jeep, joined by Nico and Charlotte, and then drove them off base.

"You guys get to take equipment just whenever?"

"Only in special cases," Nico said with a laugh. They headed onto the main highway back into San Diego, and she gave him her address, but Nico had already memorized it. A beep came from his phone, and Nico read the text and nodded. "We're clear." When they pulled up in front of her small brownstone townhome shortly thereafter, Nico looked at it in surprise and said, "This is a wealthy area of town."

"My books do fine," she said as she hopped out and looked around. She wanted to scream with joy. She was home; she was safe, and it would be a beautiful day. She ran up the steps only to have Nico intercept her. She frowned as he stepped between her and her front door. "What?"

"We'll go in and check it first," he said.

She planted her hands on her hips, feeling her temper spike. "I've come a long way to be home. Why on earth would you even begin to think that my house needed to be searched?"

"Because our team found bugs in it before."

"Bugs?" she asked cautiously.

"Bugs," he said, "as in listening devices."

She stared at him in shock, the color falling from her face. "What are you talking about? How and why would anybody plant bugs?" She tried to breathe properly. "And maybe a better question is," she asked when she could, "why on earth would they care what I say?"

"That's what we have to find out." He took the keys from her fingers, quickly unlocked the door, and then, with a nod to Keane, stepped inside. She went to follow, but Keane put his arm across the doorway, barring her from entering. She turned and glared at him.

He gave her a lazy smile. "Not until we say so."

She wanted to stamp her foot on the floor, like a child, but that was as much about exhaustion and frustration from what had gone on for the last few days. "I get that you guys are trying to protect me, but I'm home. This is my home."

"So you planted those audio devices yourself?" he asked curiously. "Just what do you listen to then, if that's the case?"

She glared at him. "You have to be mistaken."

"No, I don't think so," he said.

Just then Nico came back and opened the door. "It's clear."

She rolled her eyes at him as she sailed past him. "Of course it's clear. Remember that part about it being my home?"

"Remember that part about bugs?" Nico plunked down his bag on her kitchen table.

"I think you guys are the ones who messed up with the bugs," she said. She didn't have a very large place, but it was more than enough for her. She headed straight for the coffeepot.

"You won't sleep tonight if you have more coffee."

"Yes, I will," she said. "Coffee right now is good."

"Can you explain the bugs?"

"No, I can't," she said. "Of course I can't. Nobody gives a crap about what I say or who I say it to or when."

"Well, somebody does," he said. He walked over to the kitchen counter and lifted the one device left behind for him to identify. He held it up for her. "This is one of three."

He watched as the color drifted off her face again. "I don't know what those things are," she gasped. The reality of seeing it versus hearing about it was just too much. She sagged down to the kitchen chair and buried her face in her hands.

"I'm sorry," Nico said, "but we really do need to get to the bottom of this."

"You keep saying that," she said. "How's it going though?" There was a snappiness to her tone that she didn't mean. She pinched the bridge of her nose, then said, "I'm sorry. I have no reason to snap at you guys. You've been nothing but easy to get along with, and you've done everything to keep me safe. I'm being an ungrateful brat."

"You're tired. You're fed up, and you're frustrated," Nico said. "The bottom line is, I need to know who would come through your house on a regular basis."

"Nobody," she said. "I live a fairly loner lifestyle."

Instead of taking that for an answer, Keane dropped a pad of paper in front of her along with a pen. "Write them down," Keane said. "And hopefully you're being honest, and the list is damn short because, like you, we're also tired."

She winced at that reminder because the two men had been on just as difficult of a return journey as she had, somewhere around thirty hours of it to stay under the radar. The good thing about all that was she regained some of her Saturday, what with the time zone change from Sydney back to San Diego. She nodded and wrote down the few friends she had, and, at the very end, she put down Maggie's name. "She works here, of course, so she's another one."

There were only four names.

"No boyfriends?" Keane asked.

"No," she said, "not currently."

"Any past disgruntled boyfriends?" Keane asked.

She shook her head. "No, I still haven't moved on from my husband," she said.

"What about his family?"

She shrugged. "I don't have anything to do with them."

"And nobody else that's upset with you outside of the industry that you're always protesting against?"

She shook her head. "No, that causes me enough stress and strife. I don't need more."

"Right." Nico picked up the pad of paper and marked a line through the middle of them and said to Keane, "Half for you and half for me." And the two men set up their laptops and got to work.

"IT WON'T HELP you," Charlotte said in exasperation. "Absolutely none of those people would have put bugs in my house."

"Maybe not," Nico said, "but somebody close to them might have."

That stopped her in her tracks.

He glanced over at her and smiled. "You going to crash?" But he could see the restless energy eating away at her. She was tired, restless, and needed something to do that she could jump into. "Why don't you make some coffee," he suggested. "For us. I still don't think you need any caffeine."

Her quick frown in his direction made his grin widen.

"No, you don't have to feed us and give us coffee," he said, "but we do work better that way.'

She raised both hands in frustration, stormed over to the counter, and readied the coffeepot to brew, as he returned to his work.

Nico was much more concerned about this assistant of hers, this Maggie. The fact that Charlotte's previous assistant had died in a hit-and-run was suspicious as hell. It also had opened up a vacancy. This Maggie person was conveniently on hand to fill it. Yet it could be just luck and timing, if she'd truly needed a job.

"What's her address?" he called out. Charlotte didn't even pretend to not know who he was talking about. She spouted it off, and he realized it was just a few blocks away. "So does she walk to work?"

"Usually, yes," she said. "Lots of times she works from home and then comes here for meetings—or sometimes she comes here, and we do a bunch of work for the afternoon. Then she picks up stuff that she can take home again and returns there." Charlotte walked to the table and pulled out a chair and flopped down beside him. "It's an arrangement that works out really well for both of us."

"I can't imagine having an assistant in my house," Keane said.

"I wasn't a big fan of it at first," she said. "It works much better this way, when she's here for part of the time and then back at her place for the rest of the time. I still want privacy and peace just to be alone."

"There is something very odd about having another person in your space, when it's not a spouse or family member," Nico said.

"Not really. Plus, it's work," she said with a laugh. "And I'm trying to do my own writing, and it's hard to do that if she's here, interrupting me every five minutes."

"Do you need an assistant?"

"If I reduce a lot of my overseas visits and attending rallies and being a speaker," she said, "I would need much less help."

"And would that bother her?" Keane asked.

She looked at him in surprise. "I don't know. I never thought about it."

"Well, maybe you should though," he said in exasperation. "What you're saying now is that you're contemplating removing this person's way of making a living."

She stared at him. "So now I have to be responsible for her life too?"

Keane shrugged. "No, but, if you had her only for six

months, and she's looking at this as more of a long-term gig, she won't be impressed if, all of a sudden, she's out of a job."

Charlotte sat here with her arms crossed but her fingers moving, as if playing the piano on her arms. "I don't like the sound of that," she announced.

"Which is why a lot of people hire part-time or online assistance," Keane said. "If you only need them for ten hours a week, then that's what you pay them for."

She glanced at him in surprise. "I hadn't really thought about hiring anybody online before, but I can see the advantages."

"In this case, Maggie's personally in your face and in your home. It could be hard for her to withdraw."

Charlotte shook her head. "I don't quite understand why though," she said. "We're just employee and employer."

"I thought you were friends," Keane said quietly. As she turned to look at him, Nico watched the two of them interact. Keane's gaze was intent, as if searching for something. Nico had a lot of respect for Keane's assessment of human behavior and personalities.

She looked completely bewildered at the concept. "Of course we're friendly," she said. "But I wouldn't count her as one of my friends. She's my assistant."

Keane's lips quirked. "I wonder how *she* would describe the way the two of you were."

"I don't know," she said. She pulled out her phone and then said, "I'm supposed to check in with her."

"How about you don't just yet," Nico said, reaching for her phone.

She stared at him. "Why not?"

"Because she's likely to say something to somebody else," he said. "And, so far, we want to keep your presence at home a secret."

"I don't like keeping secrets."

"I know," he said. "But there are times when it's very important that we do keep things quiet. This is one of them."

She put her phone down on the table, hopped up, and paced about the kitchen. "This is back to you thinking that Maggie might be involved."

"No," Nico said, "it's back to keeping things close to our chest, so we don't confuse the issue with lots of other people knowing stuff when they don't need to know just yet. Let's clear all these people and see if we can come up with other suspects. Because the bottom line is, you were still kidnapped, and two of your kidnappers are dead, and one's in custody, and bugs were found in your house. What we don't know is how long they've been here."

Keane raised his head and looked over at Nico. "Good point," he said. He turned toward Charlotte. "When was the last time you were gone from the house?"

At that point, she was at the far end of the kitchen by the coffeepot. She spun and stormed back toward them. "I go out for coffee a lot. Sometimes I take my laptop and work in the coffee shop."

"They wouldn't need more than an hour or two to install these, so even that could have been enough of a window for them to have completed this job. But, just in case, when was the last time you left overnight?" Keane asked.

"At least six months ago," she said. "But that would be even worse because it would mean that the bugs were here all this time."

"And what was the start date for when Maggie worked with you and when was the first day that Vanessa worked with you?" Nico hesitated, then added, "And the last day she worked with you."

Charlotte took a slow deep breath and walked over, then picked up a laptop that she had in a fancy huge wardrobe-type cupboard and brought it back to the table where she sat down and opened it. "I did hire my newest assistant, I think within about three weeks of the previous one not showing up again."

"And so, in the meantime, you did all the work yourself?"

"In the meantime, I did none of it," she said simply. "I just let it build up. And that's when I realized I couldn't continue without an assistant."

"And did Maggie start working from your home?"

"Yes." She nodded. "Only over time has she been slowly taking some of the work back to her place."

"Do you pay her full-time?"

She nodded. "But I'm not sure I need full-time. That's a discussion I'll have to have with her."

"Did you make that as a potential down the road when you first hired her?" Keane asked.

She looked up and frowned at him. "Do you really think that she would have had me kidnapped to stop me from reducing her wages?"

"Put that way, it sounds pretty foolish," he said. "But I'm trying to get an idea of what makes her tick. Maybe she wants part-time, and maybe full-time was too much for her. I don't know."

She groaned and sagged back. "Sorry. I don't mean to be bitchy. I'm just … This whole thing is particularly unnerving."

"And that's why I wondered if you needed to have a

nap," Nico repeated.

"I slept so much on the flights that now I'm just feeling frustrated." At that, she hopped up and filled three coffee cups for the three of them. When she brought them back, Keane looked at the cup in her hand and said, "Maybe you shouldn't be having any. You're already very jittery."

She gave him a flat stare which let both of them know that anybody who tried to take away her coffee from her would pay for it.

Nico really liked that spirit and spunk. He hadn't seen enough of it, but now that she was back home again, and they were trying to solve this problem, he quite enjoyed seeing that part of her personality show up.

CHAPTER 9

THE COFFEE WAS more of a prop than a necessary stimulant because, right now, Charlotte's body was buzzing. Irritation was the primal reason. She hated all the references to Maggie being involved. But, as Charlotte sat here, being honest with herself, she was considering whether, in any way, Maggie could be involved or not. What did Charlotte really know about the woman? Then Nico started asking similar questions to what had already been in her mind.

"Is she married?"

She shook her head.

"Siblings?"

She shrugged. "I don't know."

"Children?"

"I don't know."

His eyebrows rose at that. "How long has she been here in town?"

She glared at him. "I don't know, several years at least."

He settled back.

She didn't need him to say anything to realize that basically she didn't know anything about Maggie. "It's still early in the investigation," she announced. "Why not turn your attention to somebody else?"

"Why?" Keane asked under his breath. "This one looks

really good."

She glared at him.

He gave her a half a smile and said, "We have to be realistic here. Essentially you don't know very much about this woman."

She sank back into her chair and shook her head. "I thought I did."

"And what would you think that you know?" Nico asked.

"She's caring. She's efficient. She's punctual, and she does the job I need her to do." She frowned as she tried to think about her. "She's pleasant and easy to talk to. I don't know. She has more of a grandmotherly look, and I find her somebody easy to have around." Even she could tell that those were completely inane reasons. "Look. I'm not very much into business mode apparently, and I'm doing so much less on the activism front now, and this last trip was proof that I don't want to do any more traveling either. So obviously I'll need a whole lot less of an assistant than I had before." She frowned at that. "Maggie probably only does about half-a-day's job for me anyway."

"And yet you are paying her full-time?"

She thought about it and said, "Yes, I guess I am. And that needs to stop too." She hopped to her feet and paced again. "I think I felt sorry for her."

"Uh-huh," Nico said. "That works for a lot of people."

"What? Feeling sorry for somebody? She's done a good job since I've had her here. It's not like I've regretted hiring her. But I don't need anybody for as much work anymore. A few weeks ago I decided I only wanted somebody in the house half time, so she was taking work back home again."

"But what kind of work?"

"Contacting other activists, dealing with all the emails, dealing with the publications and the government crap that seems to never end," she said. "But, if I go to just writing, then I can get rid of all that in my life. … And it's a huge headache honestly."

"But you have a huge following for your activism."

"Sure," she said. "But it's not me, it's the whole group. If I were to step out, there wouldn't be an issue."

"Whole group?"

She looked from one to the other, as they both stared at her in confusion. "Well, it's not just me who goes and does all this. There's a group of us. The GA group." They immediately wrote this down. "It stands for Global Awareness," she said. "Four of us are leaders. We had to replace two others, our right-hand guys essentially, and I guess I'll be the third. But others are stepping into our places."

"The names, please."

She quickly gave him the names of the main players. "There's Steve Darwin, although he's backed out for health reasons. There's Hank Mullins and Midge. Midge—" She hesitated. "Midge Hennessy, I think."

"And you're the fourth?"

"Yes." Then she leaned forward and tapped the pad of paper. "And the two new ones are Michael Ruse, and I believe her name is Kat Simcoe. They replaced John and Sue. John Edwards and Sue … Carlson." Again, with those names written down, she nodded and said, "So, if I step back, it's really not a big deal."

"So, when you say you have all this work that you've hired an assistant for, it's mostly work for the GA group?"

She nodded. "I do a lot of the secretarial work for the group."

"But *you* had hired this person, not the group?"

She frowned and nodded. "Yes. I did that to make my work easier so I could write. But it's not enough," she cried out in frustration. "I still don't get enough time to write."

"So who would take over the secretarial work if you step out of the picture?"

"I have no idea," she said. "It's really not my issue. I can hand it over to whomever is willing to take it over."

"But then your assistant won't have a job at all, right?"

"Probably not." She dropped her face into her hands. "Honestly, I didn't even think about this when I hired her. I was trying to replace my assistant. A big stack of work had built up. I wasn't even thinking down the road, but, after these last few days, I don't want to be doing this anymore. And that means I'm stepping back," she said firmly. "That decision is now made, and that means I have to let go of my assistant sometime in the next little while, but first I need to hand over the paperwork jobs to the new secretary."

"Who hasn't been picked yet, correct?"

She nodded. "That person hasn't been chosen because nobody knows that I'm stepping back."

"Most would say it's understandable after what you've been through."

"Maybe," she said. "But they're all fairly fanatical. I wasn't really even thinking about stepping back, but I noticed that I had been distancing myself a lot in the last six months to a year. Handing off a lot of stuff to my assistant, happy to pay somebody else to deal with it. It hasn't changed my beliefs at all, but one can keep doing only so much on this before it impacts the rest of your world, and I really, really want to get back to writing. Like I said, I think I can do a much better job reaching a wider audience through my books."

"Okay," Nico said. "How many of these people have been in your house?"

She looked at him in surprise. "Well, none of them," she said. "Or they'd have been on that other list."

"So have you met any of these other people in the group?"

She nodded. "Oh, absolutely. Lots of them. But all at events. I feel like I haven't explained this very clearly to you." And even that seemed to come out more garbled than she was expecting. "I must be more tired than I thought."

"I'll put it down to tiredness," Nico said. "And maybe, instead of that coffee, you should go lie down."

She stared at him, but even her eyes were starting to blur. "I'll lie down on the couch," she said. "Just have a nap and see if I can hit refresh on my brain."

"That sounds like a good idea. We'll keep working on the names you gave us."

She nodded, stood, picked up her coffee, and went into her living room. Her house had an open layout concept, and the change in flooring showed where the living room was. She had a gas fireplace and two couches on either side with a coffee table in the middle. She placed her cup down and snagged one of the folded blankets over the back of the couch and stretched out there. Then she pulled on the blanket and tucked it up to her chin. She closed her eyes and tried to rest.

She'd been with this GA group for a good eight years or so. She couldn't see any of those members having anything to do with this mess in her life. But no doubt somebody had arranged or screwed up the booking in Australia. It didn't make any sense though to send her over there to get kidnapped when she could just as easily have been kidnapped here.

"So why not here?" she muttered to herself.

"Are you talking to us?" Nico asked. "I thought you would be asleep."

"I'm trying to," she said. "But it makes no sense for anybody in the GA group that I'm involved with to send me to Sydney to get kidnapped. It would be much easier to attack me here."

At that, he lifted his head, looked at her, and said, "Good point. So did you have any contacts in Sydney? Did you have anybody over there particularly who would be trying to get a hold of you? To get revenge on you or something like that?"

She shook her head slowly. "I don't know why. I hardly know anybody in Sydney." It was hard to keep the bewilderment out of her voice because, damn it, she was surprised and shocked and horrified by all this. It made no sense. "I wonder if laws are more lax over there?" she asked.

"Depends on which ones you're talking about," Nico said. "Or was it just a case of it was easier because it wasn't in the States. Maybe somebody couldn't get here to get at you."

"What about the four somebodies?" she asked with a yawn. "When you think about it, two men lost their lives, and one lost his freedom over there, and one's still alive and all for what?"

"I don't know," he said. "That's what we're still working on."

"Back to that whole family thing again," Keane said. "Are you sure you don't know anything about your brother?"

"Nothing since grade four," she said, her eyes falling shut. "But feel free if you get some information to fill me in."

"Will do," he said.

She was just about to doze off when her eyes opened wide. "That's several times you've mentioned him. What do you know about my brother?" She sat up, the blanket falling off to the side as she stared at the two men. "Do you have information that I don't know?"

"Maybe," Nico said. "But it's classified."

She snorted at that. "Classified? Well, isn't that a typical government response."

He stared at her. "That's your prejudice showing."

"Prejudice?"

"Antigovernment beliefs."

At that, she stormed to her feet and asked, "Do you have any idea how little they care about the environment? How little they care about the indigenous people?"

"I'm not getting into that," Nico said. "I'm trying to tell you that you need to be a little bit more open-minded in this case."

She frowned at that. "Is my brother alive?" she demanded.

The two men exchanged looks.

She walked toward the men in the kitchen and then slammed her hands down on the table and glared at them. "Answer me, damn it."

Nico seemed to make a decision, then he nodded. "We believe so."

"Well, that's good," she said. "So you know just as much as I do, which means we believe he's alive, considering he was alive when I saw him in grade four."

"Yes," he said, "but I can't tell you very much."

"Why not?" she asked suspiciously.

"Because I don't know very much," he said.

"Well, I want somebody here who does know something," she snapped. "This is just too ridiculous."

NICO AGREED WITH her. The fact of the matter was, there was no reason that she shouldn't have access to her brother. Sure, her brother might be in some top secret world, but that didn't mean he couldn't at least communicate and let his sister know he was alive. Nico had mentioned this once more in his chat window, and it came back with a question mark. Time to remind them again. **Is it wrong for a phone call at least or have him just show up at her door?**

We'll see.

"Even if he is alive," she said, turning to face him, "that wouldn't have anything to do with this nightmare." At the odd silence again, she frowned and said, "I feel like we have a great big chasm between us, and all the information I need is floating down at the bottom."

Nico looked at her unhelpfully. "Our hands are tied too," he said.

She groaned. "You're accusing a group that I've worked with for years and my own assistant who comes into my house and here you know information about my family that I don't have any access to," she said. "And yet you want me to help you."

"I think you've been living out in the cold too long," he said quietly. "Just because I work for the government doesn't make me a bad guy. Just because you're an activist doesn't make you a bitch."

She gasped at that. "Is that how the rest of the world sees

me?”

"Activists have a role to play in this bigger world," he said. "But you can't just pigeonhole everybody as black-and-white in this scenario."

"I know that," she said. "The trouble is, I don't know what I'm supposed to do right now. You're tearing apart my world, and I don't like it."

"Of course you don't like it," he said. "Who would? But the bottom line is, somebody kidnapped you. Do you want help sorting this out or not?"

She sat down beside him. "You're making me crazy," she said.

As she reached for his coffee cup, he moved it out of her way. "Go lie down again," he ordered.

She glared at him and looked at his coffee cup, then back up at him. "Seriously?"

"Seriously," he snapped. "Get up, go over to the couch, and lie down."

"I'm not a dog," she said.

He growled, stood, and swept her into his arms, then walked into the living room and gently laid her down. He pulled the blanket back over her and said, "Now sleep." And he turned and walked away. He knew she wouldn't likely stay, but it's what she needed. She was alternating between reasonable and unreasonable, and that went along with exhaustion and all the rest of this adrenaline butt-kicking scenario that she'd been through. They would get along much better after she'd had a nap.

Nico turned around to see if she was up and ready to come after him again, instead he saw her curled up in a fetal position with her eyes closed. He glanced at Keane, who stared at him with an odd look in his eye. Nico sat down and whispered, "What?"

Keane's lips kicked up at the corner. He didn't say a word and shook his head, but his grin widened.

Nico glared at his buddy for a moment and then said, "Have you gotten anywhere with those names?"

"Friends, no connection to anything suspicious. No records, not even traffic tickets for most cases."

"Let's start on the people in the group."

"I've already taken off one name."

"Good." Nico said. "One of the guys quit, Steve Darwin, who was Australian."

"Good. Contact him."

Nico went through the Mavericks databases and did a quick search. There didn't appear to be anything outside of a couple arrests for public conduct at a big rally. Nico did find a phone number. After he dialed it, he stepped outside in the backyard, so he wouldn't disturb Charlotte. When a voice answered, he questioned if this was the Steve Darwin of the GA group. "Yes. Who's this?"

He identified himself as a friend of Charlotte's. "We're investigating a kidnapping that happened in Australia. It's brought us into the activist realm," he said. "And we're wondering if you have any knowledge of death threats sent or assaults. Maybe even other kidnappings."

"I don't have anything to do with that life anymore," he said. "I was diagnosed with cancer a year ago. That's been my life since I left. What's going on?"

"I'm sorry to hear that." Nico gave a brief description on the recent events. "She was not scheduled to go at all, but the actual organizer said that she was put down due to an error between her assistant and the organizers. But then everybody was fairly adamant that she go, even though she hadn't booked it."

"That's because normally I go every year," he said. "And this year I couldn't go. So they switched out me for her. I may have mentioned that she could go in my place, and I probably completely forgot to even mention it to her. I've been a little overwhelmed with my own world. For that, I owe her an apology."

"And I'm sure she'd like to get it," he said. "She's pretty unnerved after showing up and then never making the keynote speech."

"I heard about that," he said. "I don't have a clue who would be involved in the kidnapping though. We've had dissidents at every rally. Sometimes we think it's private citizens. Sometimes though it makes you wonder if some of these big chemical companies and industrial mills and whatnot aren't following the rules and instead are putting people in to cause trouble. But to kidnap someone? I don't know. That seems a bit far-fetched to me."

"So you've never had anything like that happen at one of these rallies before?"

"No, nothing like that at all."

"Well, if you think of anything, please call me and let me know." With that, he walked inside and quickly shared the information with Keane.

"That's a complete change of life direction," Keane said. "In his case, it's quite understandable though."

"Exactly. And it explains why he walked away."

"And Charlotte wants to go in a different direction, which is also understandable, and somebody else is probably quite eager to step into her place."

"Would that somebody have her kidnapped, with no intention of killing her, just to take over her spot?"

"Seems far-fetched," Keane said. "But again I don't have a clue what these people are like. We would think the violence wasn't the way that they operated, but …"

"It's also possible they hired somebody to do the job, and the orders either got confused or somebody got a little too eager."

"Still seems far-fetched."

They got up several times and refilled their coffee cups until the pot was gone and worked their way through every name on the list. Finally Nico shut the lid on his laptop and said, "I've got nothing. Absolutely nothing."

"I know," Keane said. The two of them stared at each other for a long moment. Just then came a rap on the front door. They looked at each other and immediately bolted. With Keane on the opposite side of the door and Nico standing near the doorknob, he pulled open the door to see a man standing there and frowning at him.

"Nico?"

"Yes, who's calling? Who are you?" Nico asked. But then he knew. He recognized the facial features. "I presume you can come in."

"Well, it doesn't make much difference now if I'm in or out," he said. "But, yes, inside would probably be better."

He let in the man. Introduced him to Keane. "And your name?"

He took a slow, deep breath, and said, "My name is Joshua, a name I haven't used in many years." He looked around. "Is Charlotte here?"

"She's on the couch, sleeping," Nico said. "Come on through this way." He led the way to find Charlotte sitting up, slowly rubbing the sleep from her eyes. When she saw the stranger, she bolted to her feet, coming awake almost instantly. She walked over, then frowned at him, and asked, "Who are you, and why are you here?"

A slow grin came across the stranger's face. "Well," he said, "I heard that maybe somebody was interested in meeting me." The two men waited to see if she finally understood. But, when she didn't, Joshua said, "My name—I haven't used it in a long time though—that you would know me by is Joshua."

She stared at him in shock. "Joshua?" Her gaze was searching as she studied the man in front of her.

He nodded slowly. "Remember me?"

CHAPTER 10

C HARLOTTE STARED AT the man in front of her, but her brain didn't want to compute. "Seriously, my brother Joshua?"

He gave her that smile that she remembered, only it was so much older looking now. "Yeah," he said. "Hi, sis."

Tears sprang to her eyes, and he opened his arms. She raced into them, and the two just held each other close. When she finally could sniffle back the joy that threatened to bubble over, she said, "Seriously, if you knew I was here all this time, why didn't you contact me?" she cried out. He looked at the two men as if for their help. "You did this, didn't you?"

Nico stared at her steadily. "Are you now unhappy that you know that he's alive?"

She was stunned. "But we just had that conversation about an hour and a half ago," she said.

"But it has been several hours since we had the original one," he said. "And the bottom line is, it was time to bring him in anyway."

"I don't understand," she said. She couldn't stop staring at Joshua. She had one photo of her parents, and he looked so much like their father. Her gaze kept going from one man to the others. "Why?"

Joshua answered, "Because I've been undercover, working for the government," he said. "And some threats were raised, and some alarms were set off that maybe I was compromised. And that your kidnapping might be connected."

"But that would mean that somebody would know that I existed, as your sister, that is," she said. "For all I knew, you were dead, running away from foster care and hitting the streets at sixteen and dying of an overdose."

He laughed at that. "You always did have a great imagination."

She gave him a pained look. "I imagined a million scenarios," she whispered. "But I can't say that you knowing that I was living here while you were alive and well, yet not contacting me, was one of them." Instantly she could see the sorrow on his face.

"It was for your own safety," he said. "And I know that sounds very hollow and empty, but, considering that you were kidnapped and two of the kidnappers and a lone gunman have since died, obviously there was a reason for it."

"Maybe," she whispered. "But what about before you went into the Secret Service?"

"My work was overseas mostly for another department," Joshua corrected her.

Charlotte waved her hand. "What about before you became an undercover whatever it is that you do? Couldn't you have contacted me then?"

"Maybe," he said. "But I went through a really rough childhood after they separated us. I became very suicidal, and I figured that you were much better off without me. We'd spent enough years apart at that point in time, and I didn't even know how to find you back then. I never did finish school, but I finally entered the military and found that I was on a fast track somehow, moving on up into the work I currently do. And I'm good at it. Finally being good at something was great, but it also meant that, when I went into it, I had to get rid of my true identity. It was perfect in a way because I didn't have any family. They knew that I had a sister lost in the system, but I hadn't had any contact with you for so many years that it became just one of those little footnotes at the bottom of the page."

"And you think that one of those little footnotes was read by the wrong person?"

"It's possible," he admitted. "It's really hard to have any answers. I hope not, as in I really hope not, but I can't be sure."

"And what would the bad guys getting a hold of me mean in terms of your work?"

"Blackmail's the biggest threat. I can't give you many details of the work that I do or possibly was doing," he said. "But the minute you become compromised, and you can be blackmailed, then …" He just opened his hands. "Basically that means my job's over."

She sagged down again on the kitchen chair, finding that her world had suddenly just shifted in a huge way. "I can't believe that you were so close by."

"Not really. But, once my cover seemingly was blown, the government removed me from my undercover assignment and, after being debriefed in DC, I got the message about you being here. So I came to Coronado," he said. "I landed about thirty minutes ago and came straight here."

"Then you made good on the traffic."

He laughed. "I did, indeed."

"Is it safe for you to be here?" She looked at him anxiously because the last thing she wanted to do was lose him now that he was here.

"As safe as I can be," he said.

She groaned. "This is all that super-secret spy stuff. It's not a world I know."

"No, you wouldn't. When I did see your name for the first time in the papers, your maiden name, I was shocked. I enjoyed following you in the news, but I couldn't dare reach out to contact you at that point in my career. Here you were making headlines all around the world," he said with a grin. "While you lived out in public, I lived in the shadows."

"And I get that you say you were good at it," she said, "but did you like being in the shadows?"

"It was good for a while," he said. "I'm two years younger than you, so you can imagine how many years I've been doing this."

"Time for a change maybe?"

"Maybe. I may not have a choice at this point."

"Right," she said. "I'm sorry if I caused you any trouble."

He smiled. "And I'm sorry if I caused you to get kidnapped. That can't have been very much fun."

"For me, not so much," she whispered. "But two of the four original kidnappers involved had it much worse."

"Not to mention the gunman who died," Keane added.

"And that is a concern," Joshua said. "Because, if the mastermind is killing people, they're cleaning up their tracks."

"Who would do this?" she asked.

"I was working in Russia," Joshua said. "Very close to a businessman running a lot of drugs and women through Eastern Europe. I was feeding information back to the European countries in order to track him down and to get all his various little stations, so we could take them all out at the same time. Your kidnapping event basically moved up that time frame."

"So does your government boss know you're here?"

"He knows that I'm coming to check on a couple supply houses, yes. As does my Russian boss."

"Supplies here?" she asked, her face paling. "That's pretty ugly to think about."

"It's all ugly to think about," he said. "But that doesn't mean that it's any less real in this world right now."

"So, if that was the case, and you were undercover with that big businessman, would somebody go to that effort to kidnap me?"

"Some files were stolen from one of the government offices, and it revealed some names. Mine was one of them."

"Ouch."

He nodded. "We were thinking that we were safe because nothing happened for the first couple weeks. Your kidnapping was the first indication that maybe I've been compromised. The decision was then made to pull me and the other four people whose names were leaked."

"So now you've left your undercover position, your government boss is busy hiring somebody to replace you, or are you still working with the government?"

"All the undercover take-down plans are happening right now," he said. "There will be sweeps on more than forty different locations over the next three days. It's best if I'm not even over there right now, and, as for my immediate future, I have no idea what I'll do next."

"Does it line up that maybe I was kidnapped at the same time?"

"It is possible," he said. "Because, just before you were kidnapped—maybe four days before—we found a connection to this trafficking scheme that led to an Australian group. And maybe they were a little more adamant about finding a way to get back at us. Maybe they had access and found my name and realized that they were in trouble and decided to preempt any raid on their place."

"So kidnapping me would stop you from raiding this Australian location or would stop you from turning over any of the information on them?"

He nodded. "And honestly, they aren't part of the raids that we've got planned so far."

"Why not them?"

"We didn't have a chance to even organize that," he said. "It was new information that just came in, but they had enough time to react. If they were told about me, then they could have gone on the offense, but it's hard to say. We're still waiting for answers."

"Can you take out the Australian group at the same time?"

He shook his head. "No, not at all. It takes a lot of time to set this up."

"So will you let them think they got away with it?"

"Oh, yes," he said. "But that doesn't mean we've forgotten they're there. Or how they're operating. Wouldn't hurt in the least to spend some time studying them to make sure that we pick up all their supply lines of their network. It'll spread all across New Zealand and through Southeast Asia."

She shook her head. "That's pretty big stuff," she admitted.

"We're hoping to save several-hundred-plus women," he said, "and that's without counting children."

"Oh, my God," she cried out. "That's terrible."

"Unfortunately it's also life," he said. "As soon as we cut

and destroy this network, a competing one will rise to the surface."

She rubbed a hand to her temple. "In theory, if that's what this is all about, then I should be safe in my own home, right?"

Joshua shook his head. "No, because, if anybody found out about you, then you're not safe at all."

"So what'll happen?"

"The interesting part of the plan is already in progress," he said.

"What plan is that?"

He laughed. "I have to die."

NICO UNDERSTOOD. HE also heartedly approved. "Is it time to come in from the cold?"

Joshua looked at him and slowly nodded. "Never really thought about it before," he said. "When you're busy doing this kind of work, living a fake life, you don't think about the other side of it. But, with everything blowing up, as it has this past week, I think it's definitely time for a change of career." His grin turned lopsided. "Still be in the government though."

"Understood," Nico said. "It would be nice to confirm that the kidnapping had something to do with it though. Because otherwise we're tearing apart her life here as well as yours."

"I don't see any other reason for it, unless you've found something."

"No, but that doesn't mean that we haven't missed something," Keane said. "She's pissed off a lot of companies and a lot of people."

"The GA group has," she said, turning to look at him. "Sure, I've been part of the group's voice for a while but much less this last six months or more. Feels like much longer. If this had happened a year ago, when I was much more visible, then I would have understood it. But to happen now, it doesn't make as much sense."

"But still, for the Australian human trafficking group to have gotten a hold of you would have been something they only learned about recently, right? Like you said, Joshua, you were compromised recently."

"Not necessarily," he said. "It's possible the Australian traffickers had their suspicions a while ago. I knew about the Australian link, but I didn't have any details until recently. It was just one of those countries that we knew would be connected, but we hadn't found it yet."

"Right," Nico said. "So it's possible but just not necessarily for sure."

"Exactly. And the thing is, she didn't want to go to Australia, so that would be a nebulous connection too," Keane added.

"Except her assistant insisted," Nico said. "So let's think about this. You, Joshua, know there's a connection to Australia, and Australia knows that you're an up-and-coming player in the entire trafficking empire, and they get suspicious and start investigating you. And how would they have found Charlotte?"

"Well, that's the problem," Joshua said. "Not only that but that would have been … how long ago? Charlotte, when did you agree to go to this Australian rally?" he asked, turning to his sister.

"Well, the organizers were telling everybody that I was

coming, but I hadn't agreed to go. So there was a big mess-up. I only ended up deciding to go within the last few days."

"But they had your name up on the promos on the website?"

She nodded. "For a few weeks anyway, I think." She looked over at Nico and said, "But that's something that needs to be checked out."

"I checked on a guy who quit the GA group, who is from Australia, Steve Darwin. It was his fault that your name was there. He thought you were going, and then, when it all blew up, they came back to him, but he's been fighting cancer this last year," Nico said. "So he wasn't exactly capable of going to the rally or making the speech, and the organizers went back after you again, hoping that you would come."

"Why would he offer my name?" she asked, puzzled.

"Because, when you and he were last active, you were quite visible and doing trips like this, weren't you?"

She nodded. "I was doing all of them." Then she winced. "Right. And, of course, once he got cancer and fought for his life, everything would have changed, and he would have been out of the loop. He wouldn't have known I had stepped back so much this last six months."

"Exactly. But I don't know if that timeline works for Joshua's group to have been alerted."

"Depends," Joshua said, thinking out loud. "If the Australian group had their suspicions about me for a few weeks, it's possible. But I didn't learn of this confirmation that we had this leak until only a little bit ago."

"And it would have been awfully convenient for them to have found out that your sister would be over there."

"And yet I wasn't really," she said.

"But then you decided to go, right?"

She nodded. "But again that was Maggie's push."

"So maybe we need to find if Maggie has any ties to Australia."

"Well, I can tell you right now she does," Charlotte said. "But I don't remember how long ago."

"What kind of ties?"

"I think she has family, but I don't remember."

"And how long has she been over here in the States?"

"I don't remember," she said.

Nico got exasperated. "Now we're back to the fact that we don't know anything about Maggie. While you guys sit here and reminisce, I'll go to her house and see what I can find."

"What? You'll just walk in and say, *Hi, I'm Nico. I'm investigating your life to see if you had something to do with your boss's kidnapping?*"

He stared at her for a moment. "You know what? That's not a half-bad idea. Maybe I'll get the cops to pull her in for questioning."

"Hey, you can't do that," she protested.

"Maybe I should though," he said. "Because all we're doing is operating blind, and we don't have enough answers. We need answers."

She groaned. "Fine, but I don't want you scaring her. Why don't I instead call and invite her over?"

"Except we don't want to let her know that you're home. Remember?"

She threw up her hands. "Fine. She doesn't live far from here. You can walk there and back easily enough."

"Right," he said. As he walked out the door, he turned to look at her and said, "She lives alone, right?"

Her lips met in a line as she said, "As I don't seem to know anything else about her, I can't answer that for sure. But my understanding is she does live alone, yes."

He nodded and said, "Back soon." And he turned, and he walked out. He was at Maggie's house quickly, as it was only a ten-minute walk away. But no lights were on, and no vehicles were in the driveway. He snuck around to the back and found the rear kitchen door unlocked. As he entered, the house had an emptiness to it, something that he'd already figured out. She'd likely left.

If she'd been involved in Charlotte's kidnapping, Maggie had booked it.

Nico stepped inside the kitchen through to the living room and the dining room, finding a single bathroom on the main floor. But an empty coldness remained, as if nobody had lived here for a while. He frowned at that and headed to the fridge only to have it confirmed. It was completely empty, and so were the cupboards. He raced up the stairs, but the bedrooms were completely empty too. If this woman had ever lived here, it had been a while ago, and maybe she'd moved out in a very short time. Why? He quickly sent a text to both his Mavericks chat box and to Keane.

With a complete search of the place done, he took several photographs and then slipped out the back door. There, he stopped and took several looks around. Maggie's place was like a townhome duplex with another one on the other side attached, but only sharing the garage. As he stood here looking, his hands on his hips, the curtain moved at a window on the duplex on the other side and dropped back into place. He studied that for a long moment before it occurred to him that he possibly had the wrong address. He quickly asked Keane in a text, but Keane confirmed it was the right address. And then Nico asked for who lived in the one beside it and gave the duplex number. The answer came back with a company name.

A rental?

Yes.

Interesting. He turned and walked away, not having any reason to suspect the other house closest to it except for the fact that somebody had looked outside. But then again, if it had been his place, he would have looked out too. As he got back to Charlotte's, he walked up to the front door and entered. She looked at him, and he could see the fear in the back of her eyes.

He smiled and said, "Well, I don't know who this Maggie person is, but maybe you should try to contact her because I just went through her house, and it's completely empty. Nobody's lived there for quite a while."

She slowly sagged into the chair and stared up at him. Then she snatched her phone and pulled up Maggie's contact information and dialed.

It rang and rang and rang, and he knew there wouldn't be any answer.

CHAPTER 11

C HARLOTTE OVERHEARD THE men talking about how Maggie had moved to the top of the suspect list again.

"Have you ever been to her place?" Nico asked.

Charlotte shook her head. "Originally I just met her at the coffee shop all the time," she said. "And then I hired her, and she started working here."

"Are you sure she doesn't have another address?"

"Of course I'm not sure," she said.

Keane punched away on this laptop. "She doesn't have another address," he said. "Her passport was checked leaving the country the same day you left."

She looked at him in shock. "Seriously?"

He nodded. "She went to Australia too."

At that, she sagged in place. "So she's involved? I can't believe it."

"She is apparently, yes," Keane said. "Or it's mighty suspicious that she left at the same time you did. Not only left but completely cleaned out her place?"

Nico nodded. "I've got the team contacting the owner of the duplex to see if they have any idea if she handed in a notice or not."

Just then Miles responded on the chat window and typed, **Maggie's rent is paid up until the end of the month. They had no idea the house was vacated.**

"So she left without giving notice. But the lease is up at the end of the month."

"Perfect timing on her part."

"If she's involved," Charlotte said.

"How long ago was she working for you?" Nico asked.

"It was a while ago. Months at least."

"Like eight weeks?" Joshua asked.

She stared at him. "She's worked for me for the last six months." she said.

"And that would make sense too," Joshua said as he sat down at a chair. "We had what we thought was maybe a breach about six months ago. But everybody decided that nothing had been stolen. In the meantime, we lost two of our agents."

"Wow," Keane said, "that can't be random."

"I don't know," Joshua noted. "Those two were a little more visible. Only two other names were on that list, but nothing else appeared to happen."

"Unless this is a long con," Nico said. "But it wasn't to take you out as much as to watch what you were doing."

"It's possible," Joshua agreed, "but I would hate to think that all the raids that are going down right now will end up with zero results because of this."

"Or it's just the Australian side that's dealing with that raid issue?" Keane asked.

"It's possible," Joshua said with a sigh.

"I don't know what to think right now," Nico stated. "But it does line up with the bugs placed here in Charlotte's house within that six-month time frame. And Maggie's access to Charlotte's house makes it that much easier for her to do that. Joshua, can you get any information on how the raids are going?"

He frowned and then nodded and pulled out his phone and sent a text. "If they can tell me anything, they will but most won't be public information and as I'm now compromised and out of the game, they won't volunteer the information."

"Right." Nico shook his head.

"So again we're in a waiting game," Keane pointed out.

"I'm not terribly impressed with this waiting game," she said. "In fact, it sucks."

"Of course nobody likes the waiting part," Nico said. "It does suck. But we also don't know, for sure, that Maggie is involved, so keep the faith."

"No," she said. "She walked away from me too, so I'm back to looking for a new assistant."

"You just said that you wouldn't get another assistant," Nico said.

"Right," she said with a groan. "You guys are making me nuts. What we have here is the potential for Joshua's undercover sting to have been found out a long time ago, and that's why my kidnapping happened, and they're just now working on the blackmail scheme part. Or it's completely unrelated."

"I don't know," Joshua said. "Like I said, we had two men disappear, and no other bodies were ever found."

She stared at him. "Well, I sure hope you get out of this business. It sounds very dangerous."

He looked at her and smiled. "I'm not the one who got kidnapped this weekend."

She just rolled her eyes at him. "And I still don't understand what that was all about. I get that my assistant's quite possibly connected because she's the one who just now left without telling me and had gone to the same country that I was forced to be at. So what are the chances that she's the one who wanted me there personally?"

The men sat up and stared at her. "Is there any reason why she would?"

She shrugged. "I have no clue. Apparently I don't know anything about her. Why would she care if I go to this rally or not? I know she loves Australia but not sure if she has any ties there."

"Let me ask you this," Keane said. "Just for the sake of discussion and completely off-topic, did anybody ever die in one of these rallies?"

She stared at him in shock. "Yes," she said. "We had one death a couple years back."

"And who was it?"

She shook her head. "The name eludes me right now," she said. "It was a young man."

Exhaustion had taken its toll. Even with the various naps, her brain wasn't functioning. Brain fog was a real thing, she started to realize. She just hadn't expected it to be something to deal with when she was jet-lagged and stressed. "I can't remember," she murmured. "Andy something, I think. I should remember though, shouldn't I? I should always remember those who die during something like that." She reached up, scrubbed her face, and said, "I have it in my notes somewhere."

"Do you know anything about his family?"

She shook her head. "No. At the time we were all devastated, but we couldn't do anything about it."

"How did he die?" Joshua asked, his tone gentle.

She stared at him, her mind trying to pull back to the time it had happened. "I believe there was a stampede, and, when he fell, he got trampled."

"Why was there a stampede?"

"A series of explosions—fireworks—had gone off nearby. People panicked, and it got a little ugly."

"A little ugly?" Nico asked. "Somebody died."

She nodded. "And I forgot all about that. How could I forget about it?"

"Because it's easier to forget about it than it is to remember," Joshua said. "It's a sanity-saving method that we all employ when we need to."

"Maybe," she whispered, "but it feels very much like an excuse right now."

"No, don't think that way. Were you at that rally?"

"I was, as were the rest of the GA group." She frowned. "Because we were all there, I see no reason for me to have been targeted."

"Are you sure about that?"

"No, I'm not sure about it," she said. "I just remember being devastated that somebody had died at one of these events."

"Did you have any contact with him?"

She nodded. "Yes, I did. I remember speaking to him earlier. It's one of the reasons why his face but apparently not his name is something I remembered. I was talking to him about our group and what we were hoping to make happen around the world."

"Was anybody with him?"

She shrugged. "I don't know. Not only was it years ago but there was also a crush of people, and I didn't speak to him long."

"So he didn't email you or have any contact with you other than that?"

"I'm not sure," she said, looking at him puzzled. "Why?"

"Just that, if he did have contact with you versus anybody else, it would explain why you were targeted."

"I was one of the speakers," she said. "And my name was up with a lot of the other organizers, so it's hard to say. Maybe because I was the only female at the time?"

"It could be something like that," Keane nodded. "We don't always know what happens or why somebody is chosen."

"But there is a reason," Nico said, "and that's what we have to figure out." He returned to the kitchen table and sat down. Joshua pulled out his phone and sent a bunch of texts.

It seemed like she was the only one completely out of the loop. "I guess this is a new avenue to explore," she said, "but why are we giving up on the other concepts?"

"We're not giving up on them," Joshua said, "but the timing would be difficult, and they're really convoluted."

"That would be good news for you though, wouldn't it?"

He nodded. "It would be very good news, if it wasn't connected to me. Unfortunately it still means it's connected to you, and that means your life is still in danger."

She groaned. "Nice." Needing a distraction, she looked around the kitchen and asked, "What about food?"

"Sure. What do you want to do?" Nico asked. "We can order in, or do you have anything that needs to be used up?"

It was at least something that she could do, and it would take her mind off all this. She walked over to the fridge and opened it up. She had very little in the way of fresh food because she'd gone to Australia. "I should check the freezer." And she found some leftover spaghetti sauce that she'd made a while back, and there was a lot, about a good-sized pot of that. She brought it out and put it in the microwave to defrost and put on a pot of water for pasta.

As the men continued to talk among themselves, she only half listened. Her mind had glommed onto the kid who had died. As she thought about it, she realized that she'd gone almost into a dark mode for a week afterward. She'd pretty well stayed in bed and cried her heart out but hadn't told anybody because she had nobody in her life to tell. She hadn't even had an assistant back then. But just the thought of violence coming out of one of the rallies that they had been in was pretty hard to understand.

She'd given several interviews where she'd apologized profusely and had said that something like that should never have happened, and then she'd basically gone into hiding as the organizers had been blamed as zealots and hadn't cared about the safety of those around them. And, of course, that had been a lie because she wasn't even part of the organizers. She'd flown over for the actual rally, but she hadn't been part of the security or the setup.

Somehow though her name had still been associated with it. Another dark stage of her life. Maybe that was the start of when she'd considered not doing many of the rallies. She had certainly slowed back down and cut her schedule by half, but it hadn't been enough.

Now she wouldn't do it anymore. This last trip had finished her. If she'd thought she was done before with rallies, she no longer had any doubts now. If her assistant was associated in any way with this, that was just double the reason to make sure Charlotte completely cut her ties with everything. She thought about all the conversations she'd had with Maggie now, wondering if it was possible that she was related to that boy. Charlotte didn't know if she was married or had children even. Lord she'd been friends but apparently had kept her back a bit on the friendship level.

Charlotte remembered a faded indent on her ring finger, as if there were a husband. Or had been a husband. People said things like that all the time to avoid the truth, not because they were trying to hide anything but because they weren't prepared to deal with the loss and to talk about something that had been recent. So, if Maggie had lost her husband any time in the last year, maybe she wasn't ready to talk about it. And the same would then apply to children. She definitely looked like the motherly type and should've had five or six young lads around her, grown up now with grandkids. But, as far as Charlotte knew, there hadn't been.

She walked over to her laptop while everything was working in the kitchen and brought up her notes. She remembered one of the organizers she'd spoken to on that job and quickly brought up any emails pertaining to it. "Andy Noster," she said. "That was his name. He was a Sydney native."

"Spell it?"

"N-o-s-t-e-r," she said. "He was eighteen."

"We'll check into it," they said.

She nodded and read through a bunch of emails. "The organizers weren't very happy either," she said. "They hadn't expected as many people to attend. The venue itself was too small for that number of attendees, and security had had to be brought in to help control the crowd."

"Right. Got it," Nico said.

She left him to it now that she had found the email that was bothering her and went back to the kitchen. As she thought about it though, she remembered some talk about him being an only child. She went back to her notes, since she had done plenty of research into his death at the time. And there, staring at her, was something that she hadn't wanted to contemplate. "He was an only child," she said.

"And who's the mother?"

"Angela Noster and her husband was Daniel Noster."

"So, not a Maggie?" Nico said. "Have you got an image of the mother?"

Charlotte quickly flicked through, brought up a photo, and then nodded. With a sigh of relief, she said, "It's not her." She twisted the laptop so he could see the image of the parents.

"Good enough," he said.

Smiling and feeling somewhat better, she finally left her laptop and went to the kitchen. Of course that didn't mean that Maggie wasn't still somehow connected. But chances were good it wasn't related to the death of that boy. When the pasta water boiled, she added salt and threw in the pasta. She hoped it was enough for four people. She didn't even know if her brother ate pasta, but it was too late to ask him now.

She kept sneaking looks at him, surprised—*stunned* maybe was a better word—to see him sitting here casually with the other two men. And yet he was so at home with this work. After all he'd gone through, he'd grown up into a hell of a man, and all she could remember was that freckle-faced kid who she tried to protect all the time. But he'd had a hell of a temper and always acted out. She'd turned and leaned back against the stove with the pasta bubbling behind her. "Joshua, how did you deal with all that anger?"

He looked up at her, and the smile that whispered across his face was more sad than happy. "Remember that depressed and suicidal time period I spoke about earlier?"

She nodded.

"Yeah, that was my answer when the violence wouldn't

get me where I wanted to go. I got suicidal."

"And was it all because of Mom and Dad?"

"That was a lot of it. It was the loss of the home that we'd had, and then, when I lost you too, I became very violent. Finally I came out of that depressed period. However, realizing that I wasn't hurting anybody but myself, and nothing was changing, even though I was constantly angry, they put me on a bunch of drugs to help calm me down. I finally stopped taking the drugs, and then I got very depressed again, so they wanted to give me more drugs. And I realized that the drugs weren't helping me any, so I stopped them. Yet I still hated my life and still hated the fact that our parents were gone, and you were gone, and I was all alone."

"I'm sorry," she said. "I kept asking them where you were and what happened to you and why I couldn't see you, but I never got any answers."

"The foster care system sucks," he said. "And, when siblings are separated, which they try not to do supposedly, it's almost impossible to reconnect again."

"I agree with that," she said. "I'm so sorry I wasn't there for you."

He stared at her, surprise lighting up his dark eyes. He put his phone down, stood, and walked toward her, then held out his hands. She put hers immediately in his. "It's not your fault," he said quietly. "I don't want you to feel guilty that we were separated."

"Too late," she said, tears choking her throat. "I cried myself to sleep for years. And then I got angry. And then I just became detached. It's like I put a veil between me and the rest of the world, so I didn't have to deal with too much of it."

"You've had a lot of sadness in your life, haven't you?"

"And a lot of anger and a lot of emotions I couldn't deal with," she said.

"You married?"

"Married and widowed. That was a bad deal for him and for me. And more guilt piled in on top."

"And you wouldn't feel as much guilt, except you're already carrying a lot from our childhood," he said. "I hope you don't think you had anything to do with Mom and Dad's accident."

"You know what? I don't even remember most of the details. I remember it was a car accident, and we survived, and they didn't."

"That's about the best way to look at it too," he said. "As far as I understand, it was a collision with a drunk driver. But, other than that, who knows."

She smiled. "We could find the files, I suppose, if we cared."

"When I went undercover, they were buried," he said.

She laughed. "Okay. So apparently I got buried too, didn't I?"

"No," he said. "That was the one part that they just left as a vague disappearance into the foster care system."

"We didn't have anything to do with the accident though, right?"

He shook his head. "No."

"Well, I didn't even realize I was worried about it. Apparently I was because I feel better now."

He smiled and nodded. "Life's like that," he said. "You do what you can, but it doesn't always work out."

"I'm so glad to see you," she said warmly. "Not in these circumstances necessarily, but to know that you're alive is huge."

He tugged her into his arms. She went willingly, and the two just held each other for a long time. She could feel the tears once again choking her throat. She sniffled, stepped back, and said, "I'm so exhausted that I don't even know if I'm coming or going anymore."

"And you will be until this is all finalized," he said. "But it will get better."

"And what will you do now?"

"Well, I'm done with that job," he said. "So maybe whatever I get to do next won't be quite so distant."

"That would be nice," she said. "I'd like to keep you in my life now that I know you're okay."

"I would love that."

He hugged her again briefly and then stepped back and said, "Are you feeding us anytime soon?"

She turned, seeing the pasta water heavily bubbling behind her. "Yeah, coming up." She quickly transferred the defrosted pasta sauce to a pot and warmed it up on the stove the rest of the way as she finished off the pasta. By the time she called out to the men to say that dinner was ready, she had more or less composed herself again.

With them quickly clearing off the table of laptops and papers and notepads, she got them to set the table, while she dished up their meal. And very quickly they were all sitting down and passing around a big tub of parmesan to sprinkle on top of their pasta sauce. She smiled as she sat down and said, "I can't remember the last time I cooked for more than myself."

"We've both been loners," her brother said.

"And how sad is that?" she said. "We were lonely growing up, and we ended up as lonely adults."

"Well, at least you were married for a few years," he said.

"I was, and it was a very special relationship. Tough and emotionally taxing but very special." She nodded at Nico. "Nico, you ever married?"

He shook his head. "Nope, not going there either."

"Keane?"

"No, and won't either."

She laughed. "So says you two," she teased. "Your minds will change someday."

"Maybe not," Keane said. He looked over at Nico. "This guy is ready for marriage though."

Nico just looked at Keane and snorted. "Right. With my job?"

"I don't think your job makes much of a difference," she said.

"I'm always traveling."

"Sure, but what you do is important, so the traveling is just part of it."

Nico gazed at her a little bit longer than necessary, but such a warm light was in his eyes that she realized they were talking on a completely different level. She immediately dropped her gaze to the spaghetti and started eating. It was her fault for bringing up the subject, but, at the same time, it was also a relief to know that maybe the two of them were on the same wavelength.

WITH THE REST of the meal put away and the dishes cleaned up, Nico sat back down at the table. He'd been delving into Andy's death—actually three years ago in Australia—because instinct said this was what Charlotte's kidnapping was all about. The fact that Maggie wasn't the mother did not deny a connection was here, and, if there were one, Nico definitely wanted to find it.

It appeared that Keane had the same idea. He'd asked Miles for a bunch of information from the Australian side too. And everything they'd come up with had said that Andy's death was an accident. It was hard to foresee something like that. The venue and the organizers had done everything they could to make the rally as safe as possible, but unfortunately something had gone wrong, and the poor kid had died. There had been no lawsuit afterward though. There'd been nothing.

Which was all good and dandy, but it meant that, if somebody had some festering anger or resentment or blame to lay from that accident, then they'd gone inside with those emotions, not venting them, like to a professional therapist or psychologist or psychiatrist. That was a little more dangerous in some cases. Nico shook his head. "I'm not seeing anything that connects Maggie to the Nosters," he muttered to Keane.

"No, and I'm not seeing anything that connects them to her either."

"So then what?" Nico asked, sitting back. He glanced at the reunited siblings. They were busy talking and enjoying catching up on the newest and latest in each other's lives. "I wonder if anybody else was killed or hurt."

"I did a search for that, but this was the only serious result. Somebody broke a leg, but it was fixed and fine."

"So we keep coming back to this boy."

"Yeah. He didn't have anybody around necessarily who would want to do something like this, taking revenge on Charlotte."

"Yet Charlotte's kidnapping is a pretty major event because of the extra deaths involved," Keane noted.

"I see that. I just don't understand the why of it," Nico said. "Obviously they were cleaning up so that they didn't get caught, but how do you avenge one death by killing three more?" Just then his phone went off. He pulled it out and checked the message. He hopped his feet and said, "I gotta phone Miles." He walked outside and said, "Miles, what's up?"

"The prisoner's talking."

"Interesting. And why is that?"

"He's scared," Miles said.

"Good. I'm glad to hear that."

"He figures he's next."

"Well, of course he is. That's pretty easy to determine."

"He said that they were hired to do this job."

"Right, and?"

"He seems to wonder now if it was a job that he was hired directly for, or if it was a job that somebody else was hired for, and then they were given the job."

"But that makes no difference," Nico said.

"No, the only difference is the fact that he never would have worked for this person in the first place."

"And why is that?"

"Because he's basically a mercenary."

"So that makes no sense still."

"I think our kidnapper's problem is the fact that, had he known the merc had hired him, he would have realized that the job would be terminal. And he wouldn't go there because of that."

"Ah, so our kidnapper wouldn't have worked for him in the first place, but now that he realizes who was his ultimate boss, then our living kidnapper knows he is in major trouble."

"Yes."

"So, what is he offering?"

"He said an Australian ultimately hired them."

"Well, that's a good start."

"Yes, but it's not enough."

"I know," Nico said.

"I was basically thinking that we need to keep the search centered on Australia."

"I want the search centered on that dead kid," Nico said. "It's about the only reason anybody would have something against Charlotte."

"You don't think it's the brother?"

"The timing doesn't completely work," he said. "We can't rule it out yet because obviously something else could be going on that we don't know about, but it seems like a stretch at the moment."

"But it seems like a stretch that this kid would have died three years ago, and now they're finally seeking revenge? Plus whoever hired them would have wanted all these men killed?"

"I know," he said.

"Oh, I did find out one thing though."

"What's that?" Nico asked as he went to hang up.

"The kid was adopted."

At that, Nico froze. "Yeah, so now we need to know who his birth parents were. That could make the difference. I was looking for any connection to Maggie, and I wasn't finding it. So let's find that connection there."

"And you're thinking this still has something to do with Maggie?"

"Let me tell you this," he said. "My gut says Maggie's

involved. My gut also says that dead kid's behind it. And now that you've told me that he's adopted, I'm pretty sure this will all make more sense really fast. So, whatever records you need to get into, get into them fast."

"On it," he said. "We've got connections inside the Australian government now. Let's see what we can find." He hung up.

Smiling, Nico walked back inside and turned to look at the three of them, who were all watching him. "Well," he said, "the prisoner's talking, and he said that he was hired by an Australian. The other thing is that the kid who died was adopted."

Immediately Keane's gaze lit up. "Ah," he said, and he tapped away at his laptop.

Whereas she looked at him in surprise and asked, "What difference does that make?"

"It makes all the difference in the world."

CHAPTER 12

HOURS LATER CHARLOTTE had collapsed on the couch yet again.

Not long afterward one of the men shouted, "Eureka."

She wanted to sit up and figure out what he was talking about, but she was just so damn tired that it was hard to move. She wanted to go to bed, but she'd also been the one who held off leaving because she didn't want to leave her guests down here. And, if something was going on, she didn't want to miss out on anything. But now that something was going on, it seemed like her body was moving in slow motion to get anywhere.

When she finally made her way into the kitchen, rubbing her eyes, Nico hopped up and said, "You should just go to bed."

"Sure," she whispered. "I should, but …" She sat down on the chair as he pulled it out for her. She smiled up at him. "Thanks. You'd make a great nurse."

Keane snorted at that. "He wouldn't do it for just anybody."

She was surprised to hear that, and she smiled at Nico, who tossed Keane a disgusted look. "He's just teasing you," she said gently.

He glanced at her in surprise. "Now you're defending him?"

"I must be having a good moment," she said, stifling a yawn. "Somebody yelled eureka. What was that all about?"

"That was me," Keane said, almost mockingly dancing in his seat in front of her.

She rolled her eyes at him. "So, will you tell me what that's all about or just sit there, like a rooster, who knows something nobody else does?"

"Maybe I'll do that," he said, laughing. "But all games aside …" He immediately launched into a discussion. "So the kid who was killed was adopted, and there had been several disputes when he was young between his adopted family and his original family. The adopted family won, and the birth family disappeared from sight."

"Interesting," she said. "I would probably always want to sit there and monitor how he's doing though."

"In some cases," Keane said, with a narrowing look, "that'd be called stalking."

She glared at him.

"Continuing now," Keane said. "Apparently, according to the kid's adoptive family, the birth parents had contacted him when he turned eighteen. They didn't have the benefit of anonymity because of how the adoption process had come about, so they knew who he was and essentially where he was." Shooting a look over at Charlotte, he said, "And likely had kept an eye on him from a distance."

"So the birth parents are stalkers. Got it," she said. She watched as her brother tried to hide his grin. And then she glanced back at Keane. "So, will you continue to be melodramatic about this, or will you finally get to the point?"

He sighed. "You don't have to be difficult all the time."

"How would you know?" she asked. "You don't even know me most of the time. Maybe I'm like this normally."

"No, you're not," Nico said. "We've talked to lots of people about you, and apparently you're one of the most giving and respected people in the group."

"How much did you pay them to say that?" she asked. But inside, she was pleased. She really was somebody who stepped out of her way to try to help. And that, in a way, made her fearful, and she came back to feeling guilty too.

"The birth family was rebuffed by the boy."

"Why would he do that?" Charlotte asked.

Keane shrugged. "I don't know, but it's not something that we can really judge at this point because we don't have any more information about that relationship."

"Or what the adoptive family may have said to the boy," she said quietly. "A lot of poison can be spread, and it may not have any meaning in reality."

"Exactly. The adoptive parents are still grieving and angry and have had no contact with the birth parents. They presume that they know about their son's death but haven't seen or heard from them since."

"So the contact must have been fairly recent if he died at eighteen and if the birth parents contacted him at eighteen."

"January. They contacted him sometime just after his birthday. You had the rally in March."

"So they didn't even have a chance to establish a relationship or to try again."

"Exactly."

"But still, you'd think they'd be more upset at the adoptive parents than at the organizers of the rally."

"Possibly," Keane said. "But another interesting fact came up. That rally had two main organizers."

"John and Sue," she said with a nod. "We had lots of emails and phone calls back and forth."

"Well, both of them died in a car accident after the rally. Did you know that?"

She frowned. "I remember hearing that they were in an accident. I didn't think that had killed them though."

"They both died in the hospital after succumbing to their injuries."

"Was it a long time afterward?" she asked, puzzled. "Because I don't remember hearing anything about it."

"It didn't garner much prominence in the newspapers," Keane said. "And that was the last rally you went to over there until you attended this one."

"Yeah," she said. "After that death, it was not something I really wanted to promote anymore."

"Understandable," her brother murmured. He looked over at Keane. "Are you expecting that to be connected?"

"I think that quite possibly it is, yes."

At that, she stared, comprehension slowly settling. "You think the organizers were killed because of the boy's death? And by his real parents?"

Keane nodded. "That's what I think."

"Cause of accident?" Nico asked.

"No idea. Apparently there wasn't a whole lot left of the vehicle. It went off the road, and, if it was run off the road, they don't know. Both passenger and driver were thrown out of the vehicle, hence their severe injuries. But, even though they had technically survived the crash, they would have died from the burns anyway."

"So, no way to open that investigation up or to access those files and take another look?" Charlotte asked.

"Our team's already sending those records to us," Keane said.

"And who are these birth parents?" she asked.

"We have Dave Mortimer and Ellen Flagstaff."

"Neither name means anything to me," she said.

"We're getting images too. And of the adopting family," Nico said. "Let's see who everybody involved in this is." He nodded and typed something back into the Mavericks chat box. "They're getting it."

Charlotte sat here, slumped in her chair, thinking about how devastating it must be to lose a child. But now that he had finally turned eighteen, and the birth parents had a hope of having a relationship, then he dies? "I wonder what the conversation was between the birth parents and Andy."

"According to the adoptive family, he said he wasn't ready for a relationship with his birth parents."

"Ah," she said with understanding. "If so, then basically his death caused by this rally lost them something they've been waiting a long time for, and what he had said could potentially happen down the road had been taken away from them."

"That would be a motive, yes."

She looked over at Nico. "So why did it have to happen in Australia though?"

"As a reenactment of Andy's death?" Keane offered. "Everything certainly seems to be centered around Australia and what happened there."

"Or," Nico suggested, "if the Australian birth family wanted revenge, it would make sense because they would have connections there."

"As in helicopters? Isn't that a bit over-the-top?"

"It depends if they have money, and it depends on how badly they wanted you to pay for their son's death."

"And why am I to blame? A lot of our group was there."

Nico reached out a hand and clasped her fingers. "That

unfortunately I can answer. According to his adoptive family, he was all gung-ho about seeing you."

Her eyebrows shot up to her hairline. "Seriously?"

Nico nodded. "According to the family, he was very impressed with you."

She groaned and sagged back. "So here we have adolescent worship, and, for all the wrong reasons, he shows up to a local rally where I'm a spokesperson. I speak with him briefly, for maybe less than a minute, and he gets killed at the rally, and now I'm blamed for his death?" She shook her head. "And have you found a way to disconnect my assistant from all this?"

"No, not at all. Considering she's the one who insisted you go, we have to consider that she is likely connected."

"I don't want to think of that," she said quietly. "I really enjoyed having her around, but it wasn't always easy."

"If it was a friendship," her brother said quietly. "It's what I do too. For years I made friends, but they were all for a purpose—to get me the information I needed."

She stared at him, her insides sinking. "And, of course, once she had her job done, she was done."

"Yes, now we don't have that name exiting through customs. She hasn't left Australia yet, so she should be still there. She was confirmed on a plane to Sydney, and there's no reason that she shouldn't have disembarked there."

"If she had a second ID, would she have been able to use that to get off elsewhere? So that nobody knows where the actual passenger is?"

"They'd be looking for her, in theory, if that was the case," he said. "Because you're pretty well tagged when you travel internationally."

"So, we can assume that she's probably still there."

"Yes."

"Wouldn't that make it a little too obvious?"

"Possibly, but you also have to consider that maybe she was planning to come over to help you, in her work capacity as your assistant."

"That's plausible," she said. "I did travel a little bit with my other assistant." She froze. "Does that mean that Maggie had something to do with that poor woman's death too?"

"We don't know, but we have to keep that avenue open," Nico said quietly.

"The world sucks," she said, hopping to her feet and walking over to the window above the kitchen sink. It was dark outside, but it was a half-lit darkness with a full moon above. "The night outside is like the world around us," she said. "You can only see that which is lit up and available to see, whereas three-fourths of what's going on around you is hidden in the shadows."

"Unfortunately that's quite true," her brother responded.

She looked back at him. "Are you allowed to be here?"

"I am right now," he said. "I was hoping that maybe I could stay for a couple days. I don't really have any other place to go. But, if it's not convenient, that's fine too. I'll grab a hotel."

She stared at him in shock. "How could it not be convenient? I haven't seen you since how many years ago, and you show up on my doorstep and then think you're not welcome?"

"In many cases like ours, I wouldn't be welcome. People would be too angry to see past the fact that I could have contacted you many years ago."

"Yeah, you could have," she said quietly. "But I'm willing to trust that you felt you were doing what you needed to do.”

He gave her a ghost of a smile. “I'm glad you feel that way. I'm not sure I can excuse it. But, as I look back, I wasn't in any great frame of mind.”

“No. I went through some of the harshest years of my life after my marriage,” she said. “And, if you had contacted me then, I might have been so angry that I would have closed the door in your face.”

“That bad? Were you abused?”

She shook her head. “No, nothing like that. It was just a very difficult time.” She gave him a brief synopsis of what happened. “But, as I've explained to the others, I've carried this massive load of guilt ever since.”

“Well, hopefully you'll get rid of it now and do the things that you need to do for you and not that you feel you have to make up for something that you didn't do.”

It was a bit convoluted, but she got the gist. She smiled at him. “Wouldn't that be nice? As I look at it, I see my guilt and so many things that I do were trying to make up for not being the perfect wife and for feeling like I was angry at the circumstances.”

“Time to let it go then,” he said quietly.

She glanced at the other two men, their heads buried in their laptops again. “Do I have to go back to Australia?”

Both looked up at her in astonishment. “Why would you do that?”

“To flush out the killer,” she said. “Or are we expecting them to find us here?” The two men exchanged glances, and she sagged back down into the same chair she had just vacated. “You're expecting an attack here, right?”

“Not necessarily,” Nico said quietly. “A part of me would much prefer that it's on home soil, where we know your space, whereas, if we're in Australia, we're in their space."

She nodded. "Still sucks."

"It does. I suspect that, with everybody looking for the birth parents so we can at least question them, we should have more answers soon though."

"And is anybody searching for my assistant?"

"The minute she crossed through the airport gates in Australia, she was tagged."

"In what way? I don't like just being a sitting duck."

"Maybe not," he said. "But at least now you're aware you're one."

CHARLOTTE COULD BARELY stay awake but was fighting going to bed.

Nico understood it, but, at the same time, it would be better if she would go to sleep. He glanced over at Keane and said, "Are you okay to take first watch?"

He nodded. "It's eleven o'clock now."

While the two men wrangled over dates and times, the brother looked on. He spoke up once and said, "I know you guys don't know me, but I'm willing to take a shift too."

Keane jumped in and said, "We appreciate the thought, but …"

Joshua nodded. "It's what I expected." He looked at his sister. "Do you have enough room?"

"Yes," she said. "It's a three-bedroom house. Come on. I'll show you to your room." She led the way, and her brother followed.

Keane and Nico looked at each other.

"I'll take that first watch," Nico said suddenly.

Keane looked at him. "Why is that?"

"I don't know," he said. "This place doesn't feel right yet."

"Good enough," Keane said. "I'll crash on the couch. I'm pretty tired."

"There's a bed upstairs. Maybe you'd sleep better."

Keane frowned and shook his head. Then he kicked off his shoes and walked over to the couch where Charlotte had been, and he crashed. Nico watched, and, within a few minutes, his friend's chest rose and fell in a deep and sturdy pattern, and Nico knew Keane was just a hair away from being out. Nico got back to his notepad. He would relish this time to take the thoughts in his mind and put them down on paper. He was pretty damn sure the assistant Maggie was behind all this, but, if she was in Australia, then she was out of the picture, as far as an attack on this house.

Maggie would have to hire somebody or have somebody already in place here as a contingency plan. Nico liked that idea. He worked away as the evening passed. And, surprisingly enough, when he checked his watch, only an hour remained before switching shifts with Keane. To keep himself awake, Nico got up and walked around a little bit, stretching his arms.

Then he checked all the windows and stepped onto the back patio and looked out at the small garden. It was a nice-enough place, if you weren't raising a family, but he would want more room and space from his neighbors if he had a choice. He stepped back inside, not sensing anything wrong out there, and headed upstairs.

One door was closed, and he presumed that was Joshua's room. Nico was still uneasy about Joshua, and it had been a little too convenient to have him show up as Charlotte's brother. But the Mavericks chat window had sent photos and confirmation that Joshua was who he said he was, so Nico was willing to put that to rest.

At least for the moment, as long as Joshua was on the right side of the law and wasn't a hired gun for the adopted family. That would be a stretch, wouldn't it? But it was also very convenient placing.

Nico shifted, looking into the empty spare room, and walked over to a window to check the world outside. But it was dark, and, outside of the city lights up and down the street, there wasn't a whole lot to see. Charlotte's door was also closed. But he opened it and poked his head in to make sure that she was sleeping here. She had pulled back the covers with just a sheet over her. She laid stretched out with one long and shapely thigh gleaming in the moonlight. He swallowed and quickly shut the door.

As he made his way back downstairs, he put on the tea-kettle and grabbed some lemon from the fridge and made himself a bracing hot lemon drink. He preferred some alcohol in it, but tonight wasn't the night for that.

For the next hour, time seemed to pass slowly. But he didn't really notice as he leaned against the countertop and mulled over the options here. Waiting for people to be picked up was more than irritating. It was daytime in Australia. Surely the cops had some news. He went back to his laptop and quickly asked again if they had heard anything from their Australian counterpart about locating the birth parents, and the chat window came back with a no. He swore, then typed into the chat box, asking, **What's taking so long?**

Hang on, the chat box texted suddenly. And just then

his phone rang. It was Miles.

"What's up?"

"They just found the birth father. He hasn't had anything to do with his son since he lost the battle to keep him. He's now a businessman and had figured that maybe his son would contact him when he was an adult. But, more or less, he just remarried and has a new family and hadn't so much ignored the fact that he had a son but had realized there wasn't anything he could do about that situation, so it was put to rest."

"But did he know his son was dead?"

"Yes, and he was sad about that, but he didn't seem to be too upset."

"What kind of business is he involved in?"

"Import and export." Miles's tone was dry.

Because, of course, that covered so much and not necessarily good or bad. "Does he own a helicopter?"

"No, he doesn't own one, but he does lease several for business purposes."

"And has he ever leased from Sky-High, like the helicopter on the top of the hotel building?"

"Yes. But then he also said that he uses several other companies as well. The report we got says that that was checked, and he does lease or use the services of other pilots as well."

"So it could have been his chopper rental up there, but Charlotte's kidnapping could have had nothing to do with him."

"Exactly."

"The birth mother?"

"He has no idea. He hasn't seen anything of her in a long time."

"Define a long time."

"He says since their son's death. They both attended the funeral from a distance."

"Ah, that's why the adoptive family didn't see them."

"Yes."

"And he says there's been no real contact since then?"

"Yes."

"Does he have any idea where she is?"

"He didn't say so. He said he had an old phone number for her. He did give it to us, and, when we called it, a message says it's been disconnected."

"Of course it has. So he doesn't know if she's alive or dead?"

"No."

"Interesting. So the father is not likely, but we can't rule him out because of the helicopter connection and because of his business."

"Exactly."

With that, Nico hung up and wrote down notes, and, just when he was done, Keane sat up.

"Did I hear that correctly?"

"Yes," Nico said, "but we're still trying to track down the birth mother."

"Are you thinking that Charlotte's assistant was the mother?"

He looked at him and said, "I like that as an idea, but now we have to prove it. Do we even know if the ages work?"

"I don't know that either."

Nico quickly typed it into the chat window. When the answer came back, his eyebrows shot up. "Interesting. The father is young, considering the boy died three years ago at the age of eighteen, making him born twenty-one years ago now. The father's only forty now. Apparently his son was born when the father was about nineteen, when the parents were both teens, I presume. That was one of the reasons they lost custody."

"So she is?" Keane asked.

A text beeped and Nico checked it out. "Thirty-seven," Nico said, now that that answer had come through.

"And Maggie the assistant was how old?"

He looked at his partner. "Charlotte said the grand-motherly type."

"Which could mean anything. Do we also know if she wore a disguise and how good she might have been with makeup?"

He sat back, thinking about it. "It's a whole lot easier to look older than younger. Let me talk to the landlord."

"Good luck with that. Did you check the time?"

He swore. "Yeah, that won't work, will it?" But then he thought out loud, "I'll ask Miles for some ID on her." He quickly opened up the chat box again and wrote down what they were thinking now and typed, **Do we have any photo ID of Maggie?** As the pictures came in, they all made her look like she was in her sixties. "Looks like she is in the area of sixty."

"So not likely the mother."

"No. So what's the connection?"

They looked at each other, and Nico felt his heart sank. "Grandmother?" He snatched up the phone and contacted Miles. "We need to check on the grandparents. On both sides of the family."

"You really think they'd be involved?"

"Depends if Andy was their only grandchild."

It took another ten minutes to get the facts. But apparently the grandparents on the birth mother's side were dead. Andy's paternal grandfather had passed away, and his paternal grandmother herself was living on a small island in Greece at this time. There were no living grandparents on Andy's adoptive family's side, having died a long time ago.

Deflated, Nico decided it was time to grab some shut-eye. "Over to you," he said to Keane. "Feels like I didn't get anywhere."

"Well, we're knocking people off the list, if nothing else."

"Right," Nico said. He headed upstairs. Joshua's door was still closed, and Nico opened the door to Charlotte's bedroom to see her tossing and turning, obviously caught up in a nightmare. He hesitated, knowing it was a dangerous move, plus he had no business invading her privacy. But it was hard for him to see somebody in so much fear and anguish. When she cried out again, her legs caught in the sheet, he immediately stepped in and closed the door gently behind him. Then he softly walked over and sat down beside her and gently shook her awake. "Charlotte."

When she finally opened her eyes and stared at him, there was no comprehension.

"Charlotte, it's Nico," he whispered.

Immediately she sat up and threw herself into his arms. "The nightmares," she gasped. "Will they ever stop?"

"They will," he reassured her, holding her close. "Just maybe not as fast as you would like them to."

She nodded and burrowed even closer. "I'm so exhausted," she whispered. "And, every time I close my eyes, I keep waking up, tied up in the back of that damn truck."

"The laundry truck?"

"I don't know if it was a laundry truck or not," she said. "It was a transport truck."

"Right," he said. "Do you remember anything about it?"

"It was one of those refrigerator trucks," she whispered. "And the guys were all sitting down at the far end, and two of them were filling the place with smoke and pissing off the other one."

He looked down at her in surprise. "I don't remember you mentioning that before about it being a refrigerator truck."

"Was it important?"

He thought about it and then said, "Quite possibly, yes. Were they all smoking?"

"Two were really heavily. The other one, I think, might have had a smoke or two but wasn't as bad."

"Right." He frowned and pulled out his phone, even with her in his arms, and sent a message on the chat window.

"You think it's important?"

"No, not necessarily," he said. "Just tying up ends."

She nodded. "I wish this would all go away."

"It will," he said. "We just have to figure out what's going on."

"Right, and that's not quite so easy." She stretched back down again on the bed and stared up at him. "Is your shift over now?"

He nodded. "Keane is taking over."

"Would you?" and then her voice fell off.

"Would I what?"

"Would you mind lying here beside me while I sleep? I mean, only if you could sleep too."

He smiled and said, "Move over."

With a big grin, she rolled over. "If you don't mind."

"Sleeping beside a beautiful woman is never something I'd argue with."

"Ah," she said. "Hopefully you don't do it with every-body."

"No, only those who ask," he said with a chuckle.

She smiled, and, as soon as he was stretched out, she curled up against him. He wrapped an arm around her, and she shifted and tucked back up close to him.

"Now sleep," he murmured. "We don't have too much longer before daytime comes anyway."

"I know," she whispered. "I need rest."

Her voice was so exhausted. He waited until she slowly drifted off to sleep, and then he let himself close his eyes. His mind still churned with ideas, trying to figure out the puzzle and who was behind all this. More information had come up, and none of it made any sense. But still, he let himself drift off to sleep.

CHAPTER 13

C HARLOTTE WOKE UP wrapped in a heated blanket. She rolled over to see Nico snoozing gently beside her. His arms were still wrapped around her, and they'd slept spoon-style for almost all the night. She looked outside to see dawn had already come and gone, and there was bright sunshine. She didn't know how much longer Nico had before Keane came to wake him up because she thought she could hear her brother going down the stairs. Well, she hoped it was her brother. She was still overwhelmed with all that had happened in the last few days. She hated to wake Nico, so she murmured close against his lips, "You awake?"

"I am," he murmured, his warm breath mingling with hers, sending a shiver down her back and through her soul. She'd been alone for so damn long. She hadn't had a serious relationship since her husband's passing, and really she hadn't even had a light one either. Not one that mattered. Just so much in her world was different now. And it was changing yet again. She could feel it. She was done with traveling; she was done with rallies, and she would spend a more introspective time and work on her writing. She'd said it many times, but this was the first time that she really felt that deep and utter knowing inside. "Do we have to get up?"

His arms tightened around her, tucking her up closer.

She smiled and nuzzled his neck.

"Only if you want to," he murmured.

"I don't want to move," she said.

"Then don't," he said, but he yawned a moment later and shifted a little more comfortably.

She smiled. "Once you're awake, you're the get-up-and-go kind of guy, aren't you?"

"Not so much that," he said, "but waking up with a beautiful woman in my arms and not planning on staying in bed for the next hour or so isn't the most pleasant feeling."

It took her a moment to figure it out; then she shifted her hips, and, sure enough, there was a wonderfully long and hot ridge pressed against her pelvis. Her breath sucked back into her throat. She tilted her head and said, "Wow."

He didn't say anything, but the corner of his lips kicked up. "No, wow," he said. "I need to tell him to go back to sleep."

She snickered at that. "Does he follow orders?"

"No," he said, "at least never when he's supposed to."

She smiled and gently shifted her hips, her pelvis stroking that ridge.

He shifted his hips back and said, "You're playing with fire."

"And it's already so damn hot in here," she said, pulling off the blankets so that the two of them were just lying here together. And then she realized that, somewhere along the line, he had stripped down to just his boxers. And she was wearing her camisole and shorty shorts, her preferred nighttime sleepwear. Meaning, very little material stood between the two of them. She gently stroked his cheek and said, "If we have an hour, I definitely have a better idea than getting up."

He froze under her ministrations. His eyes opened, and

the longing look in them had her heart racing.

She smiled and gently kissed him on the chin and whispered, "If you're interested, that is."

He nuzzled her nose with his and whispered, "Anybody would have seen how interested I was."

"Well, I'm not the most observant," she whispered. "And I've spent the last many years turning and deflecting male attention rather than encouraging it."

"Your husband?"

She nodded and kissed his chin again. She cupped her hands to his cheeks and then stroked his ears, sliding her fingers through his curls. Then she trailed her fingertips to his shoulders and whispered, "I've been alone for a very long time."

"Well, I'm not really a member of the lonely hearts club," he said.

Her own lips kicked up. "Didn't ask you to be, did I?" She brought her gaze to his as he studied her intently.

He reached up his thumb, gently stroking her bottom lip. "I don't play around is what I mean," he said. "I'm not a big fan of hopping into bed and out of bed and warming up another woman's bed."

"Good," she said. "I figured you had more substance than that."

"Well, let's just say there are times when that's very much wanted and welcomed, but it's been a long time since I wanted a relationship where it wasn't with the same woman for several nights in a row."

She laughed. "Well, since my last serious relationship was with my husband, I'm all for a little bit more long-term."

"The question is, how long-term?"

Her eyebrows rose as she realized there was an intentional meaning behind his questioning. "Well, I'm certainly open to seeing how far it goes," she said, her breath heated and wispy as she tried to control her heart slamming against her chest. "I can't really say that I have any experience in affairs, and I'm not sure I want to have that experience, but, if I found somebody who could possibly be interested in a long-term relationship …" She let her voice trail off.

"Yeah?" he asked, flipping her onto her back and stretching out over the top of her. He stared down at her. "So, something like a long-term relationship might be of interest, huh?"

She reached up and kissed him again. In a teasing voice, she said, "Well, I would be if I thought I knew anybody who might be interested in that with me."

"Oh, I'm interested," he said. "But I don't really know what I'm doing for work."

"Well, I don't really know what I'm doing either," she said. "We're quite the pair." She looped her arms over his neck, playing with the hair at the base of his neck. "But we could take this one day at a time and see where it goes."

"One day?" he asked, licking her bottom lip. "How about one week, one month, one year, and maybe, if we're lucky, a lifetime?"

"Oh, I can get behind that," she whispered gently as he stroked her lips with his. "No doubt something is between us," she said. "I just wasn't sure if you were interested in going further."

"And I figured that it was happening too fast, and you needed time to deal with everything going on around you before I approached it."

"No," she said. "Life is for living. And, if there's one lesson I learned from my husband, it was to enjoy the good times because you can't guarantee when bad times are coming."

"But neither do we expect those times to come," he said quietly.

She smiled and nodded. "Very true, so yet another reason for taking the moments when we can get them." She cupped his cheek with both hands, tugging him ever so much lower and kissing him deeply, her tongue sliding inside to stroke and then play with his tongue.

When she went to withdraw, his head came down with hers, and his tongue drove deeper and deeper into her mouth as his hips mimicked the motion of her pelvis. She wrapped her long legs up and around his hips and ground upward. He pulled his head back, gasped, and whispered, "I'm not sure I can hold on too much longer."

"Good," she said. "Does it look like I'm asking you to extend this? I'd pick hard and fast any day."

At that, he groaned and sat up. His boxers went flying, and so did her undies. Then he stopped, sitting up, his palm coming to rest over the strip of curly hair and whispered, "You're so damn beautiful."

"I don't know about that," she said, "but, if you think so, I'm fine with it." She crossed her arms, then pulled off her camisole and tossed it along with the other pieces. He gasped, and his hands automatically cupped her breasts. She'd always thought her breasts were her best element, and that sucked because she always kept them hidden. But, as his hands cupped them, she tilted her head back, loving his caress, and just knowing that, for one moment, this man cared and truly loved what he was seeing.

When one hand slipped away down to her hip, she

crashed back down onto the bed and opened her arms. But his mouth came down and suckled one of her nipples, almost drawing the breast deep into his mouth. She moaned, feeling an answering impulse in her lower abdomen. He did the same for the other one, until she writhed in his arms. She reached down then, her hands sliding up and down his hips to grasp him in her hand. He shuddered, and she stroked him ever-so-gently up and then slowly down.

And suddenly that was too much for him, and he shifted her thighs wide and slid into position. She moaned as he lowered his head in a beeline from between her breasts and down to her navel and all the way to her curls. When she felt his tongue on her sensitive nub, she came off the bed, crying out. He came racing back up and lifted her hips, and, with his gaze locked on hers, he slid deep inside. She shuddered, feeling her body stretch to accept him.

When he was finally there, he whispered, "Are you okay?"

She nodded and said, "It's been so long."

He lowered himself over her and held her head with his hands, his fingers sliding into her hair, cupping her head. Then he started to move.

She wrapped her arms around him and hung on for the ride. With her hips completely overwhelmed at the movement, her body naturally moved. He pounded into her in a rhythm as old as time. She wrapped her legs tight around his hips and shifted her body. And there, that one spot just had her body shuddering. She cried out and arched her back, but he rode her through it and kept on driving for his own pleasure, inciting yet another wave as another orgasm built within.

She was still gasping when he shuddered above her. His

own voice got her rolling deep, and she held him close and as he spilled himself into her. Her own climax sent her over the edge, and she cried out for a third time. Her body was shaking and trembling. She couldn't even stop it. She didn't know what was going on, but it was a reaction to so much pleasure.

He made a startled exclamation and rolled over, then pulled her tight against him and whispered, "Are you okay?"

She shuddered a few more times, then opened her eyes and whispered, "Never better. But, dear God, that was intense."

He kissed her again, long and deep, and whispered, "We've probably used up all of our spare time."

She moaned. "Now I really don't want to go downstairs."

"Are you embarrassed?" he asked, his brows coming together.

She snorted. "Hell no. I just want to stay here and do that all over again."

AFTER A QUICK wash and getting dressed, Nico stood beside her, still napping in bed. He kissed her gently and said, "Come down when you feel like it."

She gave him a finger wave and said, "I'll have a shower first."

Nico walked down the stairs ten minutes later to see Keane sitting at the laptop.

Keane looked up, smiled, and said, "Have a good night?"

"The best," he said with a tactical agreement between them not to mention the last hour. He was perfectly aware that her cries had been much less than muted. He walked over and said, "Are you ready for coffee?"

"Hell yes."

He heard another man coming downstairs and assumed it was Joshua.

When Joshua entered in jeans and a T-shirt and slumped onto a kitchen chair, he said, "I'm a little lost, trying to figure out what to do in my civilian life again. I feel like I could sleep for days."

"How long were you under this last time?"

"Two years."

"And do you even want to go back under?" Keane asked. "It's not the easiest of lives."

"No, it's not," he said. "It's something I'll have to consider. It's hard to meet anybody when you're living a lie. Not exactly the way I would want to have a relationship."

"No," Nico said. "That's the worst. And yet, when you're doing the job, how can you not? It's lonely already. Did you leave anybody behind?"

"I did, and she'll be devastated."

"And how are you feeling?"

"I'd go back in a heartbeat," he said. "But I know that it can't be."

"Can you get her out?"

He shook his head. "No, I don't think so. And I'm not sure it's fair to her. That's the world she knows. This would be a very different one."

At that point, Charlotte walked in. "But, if she's not given a choice," she said, "you don't know what her reaction would be."

"True, but I don't have that option," Joshua said. He smiled at his sister. "You look better."

"I feel it too," she said brightly.

Nico studied her face, and she did look much less exhausted and almost refreshed. But then good lovemaking would do that. "I hope you don't mind that I put on coffee."

"Good," she said, "because I could use a cup myself." She sat down at the table and said, "Please tell me that somebody has a plan for today."

"At the moment, we're feeling a little bit at loose ends on some of it," Keane offered.

"Not sure yet," Nico said. "I'm waiting for a different answer too."

She looked over at him. "Why? What answer?"

"That comment you made about the smokers last night," he said.

"Right," she said. "But I don't know who that other man was."

"And you can't give us a description of him?"

"No, not really," she said. "He was older than the others. I figured he was more of the boss man. And one guy did quit smoking when he was told, but the other two didn't."

"Right." He looked over at Keane and said, "Charlotte mentioned that, when she was tied up in the back of a refrigerator truck, and the guys were at the end of the trailer, where the door is, and smoking. And one of the guys complained. What I want to know is, who the guy in jail is, which one of the two still alive out of those original four kidnappers."

Just then his phone buzzed. He checked it and walked over to his laptop. "Miles just sent us part of the interview with that guy, our captive." He sat down and brought it up on newsfeed.

She looked at it, sighed, and said, "I think he was a

smoker."

"Yeah, but was he the smoker who stopped?"

She looked at it, frowned, and said, "I think so."

Just then the voices filled the air, and their captive asked if he could have a cigarette.

"You should quit," the interviewer said. "It's bad for your health."

"Yeah, I know," he said. "The other two guys smoked like crazy men, and they're dead."

"And that's what I wanted to know," Nico said. He hit the Pause button, looked over at Keane, and said, "We're dealing with two separate issues here."

"In what way?"

"What if the two kidnappers were killed *not* because they failed at the kidnapping or at the handoff or whatever but because of the smoking?" Even Joshua snorted at that. But then, as Nico explained, he said, "This is the guy who stopped when he was ordered to. The other two did not."

"So, you're saying that the fourth guy is the local boss man," Keane asked, "and he is the one who we're really looking for?"

Nico nodded. "So, what we have is one killer who took out his cohorts because he was disgusted with their smoking behavior, but that had nothing to do with the kidnapping."

"So, we still have to find out who this guy is and what his relationship is to Charlotte."

"Well, his relationship is likely that he was hired, but who was he hired *by* is the real question. Probably the merc." Nico hit Play on the interview, and the same guy was being asked questions about the fourth man who didn't like the smokers.

"He's the one who hired us. He used to get pissed off because they were supposed to do what he said."

"How did he contact you?"

"I was on the street one day, smoking outside the hotel, and he came out and asked if I was interested in making some money. I didn't realize that it would get this ugly."

"What were you supposed to do?"

"I was supposed to help kidnap this woman, who was being taken to a businessman who wanted to question her."

"And do you have any idea why?"

He shook his head. "No, I don't. It didn't matter. But then killing wasn't involved."

"Do you know who the businessman was?"

He shook his head. "No, and we were told we'd never know."

"Makes sense," the interviewer said. "So, if you can't tell us who hired you, then how about the fourth guy? The one who was the leader? How would we contact him?"

"I've seen him around. He hangs at the coffee shop. A couple coffee shops actually, all in the same block around the hotel."

Just then the Mavericks chat window popped up. **We've picked up a fourth man.**

"Yes," Charlotte said, her hands on Nico's shoulders and squeezing tight. "They got him."

"Yes, and that is very good news."

The chat box texted again. **He's not talking but has been ID'd by the other kidnapper.**

"So now we have ID'd the four locals who were hired." Nico typed into the chat box, **Have forensics check this guy to see if he killed the two dead men in the apartment.**

A question mark came back.

Nico explained. **They were smokers, heavy smokers who wouldn't listen to him when he told them to stop. What are the chances that this is just a simple case of**

You work for me, so you do what I say. And, when you don't, I'll pop you one?

The word **Shit** showed up in the Mavericks chat box, and then it disappeared again.

"Which would mean that the kidnappers didn't really intend to kill me," Charlotte said slowly.

"Not these guys," Nico said. "But that doesn't mean that the one who hired them wasn't thinking about it."

"You know what? *Businessman* still takes us back to Andy's real father," Keane noted.

"It does," Nico said. On another thought, he added, "I want to know what the boy's birth mother did for a living." He typed that question in the chat box. An answer came back almost immediately.

I believe she worked in the hotel industry. Why?

Just searching for some answers. Keane raised an eyebrow at the chat box exchange, and Nico shrugged. "That might be how she connected with a merc. Maybe someone who stayed at the hotel? Or someone who knew someone. The average person isn't going to be able to pick up the phone and call for a hired killer."

With the idea that they now had the four men who had been hired to kidnap her, coffee was poured, and their conversation was animated as they came up with ideas.

Finally she got up and said, "I need breakfast. Bacon and eggs for anybody?"

Nico laughed. "Absolutely," he said. "You can feed me bacon and eggs any day."

She tossed him a special smile and pulled out the bacon and put it in the pan. He absolutely loved the domesticity of this. But, at the same time, he also knew that Keane and Joshua were well aware of the change of status in Nico and Charlotte's relationship. Tough. If they didn't like it, too bad. He was a happy camper.

CHAPTER 14

CHARLOTTE MADE BACON and eggs for everyone, while they waited for more answers. She didn't know how much of a change this was, and the fact that they had accounted for the four local men involved in her kidnapping was huge. Just then she set the plates on the table, and Nico's phone rang.

He pulled it out and said, "What's up?" After a pause, he said, "Okay, well, that's good news." He hit the Speaker button and put it on the table and said, "You're on Speakerphone."

"We have the boss man's phone, and there is proof now that it was the boy's father. He can say he had no connection to the kidnapping all he wants, but we have texts back and forth, including the amount set up to do the job."

"Woo-hoo," she said, "although that sucks big time."

"I know," Miles said, "but we're about to pick up the father now."

"Confirm when you've got him," Nico said. "We really want to know that this is over with."

"Will do."

With that, everybody dug into their bacon and eggs. She ate slower, her mind thinking about the loss that Andy's birth family had experienced and wondering how she'd feel if she had lost a child when a teenager to adoption and then to go through it all over again when the child died, finally at the age of majority to choose for himself who he wanted to be around. Because really the birth family had lost the war originally, when they were young. Even if you go on, and you have another family, surely you don't ever really forget that firstborn son of yours. "I can see how somebody might want answers. I hope they didn't want to kill me out of revenge though."

"It's hard to say. Until we get a hold of the birth parents, there's no way to know."

She nodded. "So can we go out of the house today, or are we stuck here?"

"I'm going out," Joshua said. "I have to head to a couple debriefings. I don't even know if I'll be home today. I hope so though. I don't have much in the way of gear. Everything got left behind."

"And did they kill you to get rid of you in that undercover scenario?" she asked.

He gave her half a smile. "I don't know," he said, "but I can't imagine that they left too many threads loose."

She nodded. As she got up and finished the dishes, with both Nico and Keane helping, Joshua walked over and gave her a hug. "I don't have a phone, but, if you give me your number, when I get hold of a phone and get things set up, I'll call you. Otherwise expect me back later today."

She kissed him on the cheek and gave him a big hug. "I'm so grateful to have you back in my life."

He turned and headed out to the front door.

She faced Nico and Keane and said, "Wouldn't it be nice to have this over with today?"

Keane nodded, but his voice was serious as he said, "Things generally happen fast when we get to that point."

"But, of course, it's all getting to that point," she joked.

He nodded. "Exactly."

She smiled and sat down, and, when the front door opened again, she called out, "Did you forget something?"

"Yeah, I did." But his voice was different this time.

Startled, she stared up as he came in and behind him was her assistant. Joshua had his hands up and a hard look on his face. He looked over at the two men and said, "Sorry, she was waiting for me outside the front door."

Keane swore and said, "What the hell? She must have just arrived then."

Maggie pushed Joshua to the empty chair at the table. "Sit down," she barked.

He sat down gently.

Charlotte stared at Maggie. "I don't understand," she said. "What's this all about? Maggie?"

Hate twisted Maggie's face until it was almost unrecognizable. Maggie walked over to the kitchen sink and grabbed some paper towels, got them wet, added a little bit of the hand soap that was there, all the time keeping the gun pointed at everybody. And then she reached up, with one eye closed, and quickly swiped down that side of her face, then the other. As the paper towel came away, covered in makeup, Maggie's face had turned into this nightmarish facade, half without makeup and the other half with the makeup a smeared mess.

Charlotte stared in horror. "Seriously?"

Maggie laughed. "You're such a fool."

Charlotte sat down hard. "Maybe because I wasn't looking for an enemy in my own ranks," she whispered. She stared as Maggie made several more passes with a paper towel and wiped off 90 percent of the makeup.

What emerged was a woman in her forties, showing some age. But the evil darkness in her eyes said much about who she was. "I don't give a shit what you were expecting or not," she said, "but somebody has to pay for what you did." She leaned back against the sink, this time with a dry paper towel in her hand. She wiped the moisture off her face and still more makeup came with it. She kept raising the gun when any of the men shifted. "Don't even think about it," she said. "I don't give a shit about who and what you are in any way when you're associated with her."

"How can you say that?" Charlotte asked. "I've never done anything to you."

"No," she said, "you probably didn't. But what you did to my son was way worse."

"I didn't do anything," she cried out. "What are you talking about?" But inside, she knew. Inside, she had a really ugly feeling that this was the dead kid's mum. "Are you Andy's mother?"

Maggie's face twisted. "Yes. That kid was my son! My only son! And you killed him." Her voice broke on the last word.

"I didn't kill him," Charlotte protested. "You know that."

"I don't know anything about it," Maggie said, suddenly calm.

Her moods were volatile and switching. It was something else Charlotte had never seen. Maggie had always been the most mild-mannered person. Maybe that's why she'd worked so much from home because there she didn't have to keep up the pretense. But, even now, Charlotte could see that things were unraveling. "And do you think I killed him at that rally?"

"You curried his favor. You built yourself up in his eyes so that he was so in love with you and so fascinated by who you were and what you were doing. He was on fire to do anything for you."

"I didn't even know him," she said.

Just then the gun leveled at her.

"What?" Maggie asked in a super-quiet voice.

Instantly Charlotte realized she'd made a mistake. "I didn't know him personally," she said. "I had no correspondence with him."

"Lies," she said with a wave of her hand. "All lies."

"What are you talking about?" she asked.

"I checked your emails. There were several from him. You couldn't even be bothered to answer. The poor kid was completely awestruck with you, and you wouldn't even give him the time of day."

How did that even work in terms of having a relationship if she hadn't even responded? Didn't that mean she didn't have a relationship? But she knew there was no such thing as logic anymore with this woman in front of her. "I don't remember seeing any emails," she said. "I even searched to see if there were any."

"Well, there weren't," Maggie said. "I forwarded them to myself and then deleted them forever. There are ways to recover all kinds of stuff, but I made sure you wouldn't recover these."

"So I didn't even find these emails," she said in disbelief. "But you're still blaming me for his death?"

"Well, you're responsible," the woman said in a very reasonable tone.

It was that tone that scared Charlotte more than anything. The look in Maggie's eyes and the tone of her voice were such complete opposites that it was obvious Maggie had lost whatever little bit of sanity she had. "I'm sorry that you lost him as a child."

Maggie's face twisted with fear. "Just because we were teenagers," she spat, "everybody else fought us. They took my son away and made it very clear that we were not old enough to raise him."

"And they gave him to somebody else?" Charlotte asked. She looked at the other men, but they were all sitting frozen, completely motionless. But she wasn't fooled either. They might not be moving, but their brains were as they tried to figure a way out of this. If all three of them jumped Maggie, they would definitely overpower her. But somebody would get shot in the process. And Charlotte definitely didn't want any more killings on her hands.

The woman sneered. "They gave him to friends! Family friends who had always wanted to have a child but couldn't." Her voice broke again. "I bawled and cried and screamed and went to the police. It was pretty nasty, but the police sided with my parents."

"How old were you?" Charlotte asked. "Surely they wouldn't have taken the child from the mother."

"But I was no longer allowed to stay at home," Maggie said. "And, if the child is deemed to be better off with an adopted family who would give him more of a life than I could, then everybody was against me."

"And what about the father?" Charlotte asked.

"He was screaming along with me," Maggie admitted. "But he was just a teenager, like me. We didn't have jobs. We hadn't finished school, and we were a mess. But we really, really wanted our son."

"I'm sorry you didn't have family who supported you,"

Charlotte said.

"They were embarrassed and horrified that I'd gotten pregnant out of wedlock."

"Which was also very common in those days," Charlotte said with a nod. "You might have gotten a different reception at this day and age."

"Maybe. I made a stink for as long and as hard as I could, until the adopting parents picked up and moved away, and I lost track of them. It broke my heart, and I never forgave my parents."

"Did you have to kill them though?" Nico asked quietly beside her.

Charlotte looked at him in horror and then back at Maggie. "Please tell me that you didn't kill your parents."

"Why not?" she asked. "I was glad to. They killed the most important thing in my life, which was the relationship with my son. They shouldn't have had any relationship with each other either. The world is a much better place without them. So basically you should be thanking me."

"What did you do?" Nico asked. "I never did see any reports as to how they died."

"Accidental asphyxiation," she said. "Funny how the gas overcame them."

Charlotte stared at her in shock. "You gassed them?"

"Well, I fixed their tea and knocked them out, then put them in the kitchen and just let the gas run." She smiled. "It's really easy to kill somebody, you know."

"Are they the only ones you killed?"

She shrugged. "It does get easier."

"And what about your son's adoptive parents? You didn't kill them?"

"I really wanted to," she said. "I really, really wanted to.

I saw them with my son several times, and, as much as I hated to admit it, they were really good with him. And he really loved them. And I found that I couldn't do anything that would hurt my son. I wasn't allowed to have anything to do with him until he was an adult, and I knew, at that point in time, everything that they had done wrong, I would hear about. And anything they got right, I would also hear about because my son would tell me everything."

Charlotte couldn't imagine being eighteen and telling a woman who hadn't been part of his life since his birth any of that. But maybe Charlotte was wrong. Maybe that was something that adopted kids immediately did when they were found. "Didn't you have contact with him when he turned eighteen?"

Maggie waved a hand and said, "Yes, I did, and he didn't know what he was talking about. He was just shocked."

"You mean, he didn't want to have a relationship with you?"

"Again he didn't know what he was talking about," she said. "I should have given him more preparation time. Not just sprung it on him."

"You mean, sprung on him the fact that he was adopted, and he didn't even know that much?"

Her face twisted yet again. "He didn't know," she said. Maggie stared up at the ceiling as she contemplated that knowledge. "I would have approached it quite differently if I had realized he didn't know that. As it was, he was angry at me, and I'm sure he was very angry at them too."

"But now you had opened the door, and, once he was older …"

"He said it was too soon, and he couldn't deal with it. But I knew that, over time, he would. And I always had that hope that, when he turned eighteen, I'd see him again. And, once I saw him, I had that hope that, when he had time to adjust, he'd be there, and I'd have my son back."

"But it didn't work out that way, did it?" Nico asked, his voice gentle, soft, and compassionate.

Charlotte was stunned to realize just how much goodness was in that man, that, even in a situation like this, he could sympathize and be empathetic with a woman holding a gun on him.

Maggie looked at him and frowned. "No, and that's because of the woman beside you. She's really not a nice person, you know? She took everything from me, and I've already lost so much."

"That's not true," Charlotte said. She tried hard to be calm and quiet, but her nerves were again stretched even more with the lies hurled at her. "I didn't know anything about the arrangements for that rally. I didn't have anything to do with the timing."

"Oh, so ignorance is an excuse then, is it?" Maggie shook her head. "It doesn't matter what you say. You're guilty."

"More guilty than John Edwards and Sue Carlson?" Nico asked.

The two organizers who had died in a car accident, Charlotte remembered.

Maggie looked at him in surprise. "Wow, are you police or something? Because I wasn't expecting anybody to connect that at all."

"Connect?" Charlotte asked, knowing that she had to get answers that were clear. "Are you saying that you killed the two organizers involved in setting up that rally?"

Maggie looked at her in surprise. "Well, I said people had to pay." She raised a shaky hand to her head and came away with more makeup. She stared in disgust. "Do you know how long it took to curry favor and to get you to offer me that damn job and then to get started here to find the information I needed?"

"What information could I possibly have had?" Charlotte asked.

"Well, it wasn't so much information you had, but I needed your contact information to make my plan work."

"And what plan was that?"

"Well, you needed to go back to Australia, and I needed a way to get you there," she said.

Charlotte was still trying to deal with the fact that Maggie had killed the organizers from the rally where her son had died. "Hang on a second. Go back to the organizers. How did you kill them?"

"I cut their brake line. They were going home via that nasty highway, and there were a couple really ugly corners. I knew that the chances of them surviving a trip like that without brakes were pretty slim. I didn't cut it all the way through, but you know what I mean. It's pretty easy to kill. I don't understand why people get caught all the time."

"And, of course, you didn't get caught," Charlotte said in shock. "They both died at your hand, and nobody even knew."

"Nope," she said, "they didn't. John and Sue didn't know either, which was too bad because I really wanted them to know. I wanted them to understand why they weren't allowed to live anymore and what they'd done to deserve the same fate that they gave my son."

"You do realize that they had no say either? That security was hired at the location, and it was a terrible accident."

"An accident doesn't work for me," she said, "because

that means there's no blame attached."

And Charlotte understood. "And, if no blame is attached, you have nobody to blame," she said quietly. "That's why you can't live like this, you know?"

"Well, somebody has to be blamed," Maggie said. "Who else do you have to target all that rage on if you don't have somebody to blame?"

"Well, in my case," Charlotte said, "I turned on myself and felt guilty. You could have done that yourself. Felt guilt that you hadn't warned Andy to stay away, guilt that you hadn't shown up at the rally and stopped him from being in a dangerous position, guilt for not having done more and for not telling him that this was a really bad idea."

"But I didn't know," Maggie said angrily. "How am I supposed to stop him when I didn't know?"

"I don't know. How was I supposed to save him when I didn't know either?"

The two women stared at each other at an impasse.

And then Maggie relaxed and laughed. "That's not bad," she said. "That's not bad at all. It won't do you any good, of course, but it's not bad."

"So you killed your parents and you killed the organizers," Nico said. "And then you came here, intent on killing Charlotte. Why didn't you just wipe her out on the road one day or shoot her like you're planning to now?"

"Well, it took time," Maggie said. "I didn't really know what I wanted to do. But I mean, after many deaths, this was a little special. I've been waiting for a long time. It wasn't just revenge for me. It was revenge for poor Andy. And that was important. I figured that I'd find a way to make it happen, but I didn't want it to be over here. The laws here in America are very different, so I wanted her to die in Australia. Most people won't care anyway, as she'll be just another dead foreigner."

"So," Charlotte said, suddenly seeing the light, "that's why the organizers were told I was coming. You're the one who told them that I was coming."

"Of course. It's not like you mess up something like that."

"No, of course not," she said. "And here, all that time, I believed you when you said that they were just using it as a con to get me there. But instead you agreed on my behalf. And there it looked like I was just a sore loser and pulling out at the last minute. And, of course, I would have been if I hadn't gone, and you convinced me that I needed to go."

"Particularly since Andy died there."

She shook her head. "You couldn't stand the fact that I was still living and that he was dead and that I didn't even seem to know anything about it or even care."

"You didn't care! That's the thing that I didn't get! You didn't care. How could you not care about my son?"

"Because it's easy to forget," she admitted. "When you think about it, some of this is very easy. But I never really forgot. I just pushed it away because there was nothing I could do to help Andy."

"Well, guess what?" she asked. "You'll help now by dying."

"But you haven't told us everything yet," Nico said. "Don't you want to show off everything that you've done?"

Maggie looked at him and frowned. "Sure. I arranged for her to go to Australia and to get kidnapped."

"In a helicopter?"

"I pulled in a favor. He didn't really know anything about it, but I needed that helicopter. So I used a friend's account. I thought it important that she died where my beloved son died."

"His father's account, right?"

At that, Maggie froze. Her gaze went to each of the three men. "What do you know about his father?"

"We've already spoken to him," he said. "Is he in on this with you?"

"Hell no," she said. "He's not smart enough. He already has a family and more kids too. It's me who couldn't have any more children after Andy. Something went wrong, and I couldn't have any more. And that's another reason why she has to pay." Her voice was now normal and commonplace once more.

"Seriously?" Charlotte asked. "So you hacked his email too?"

With that, Maggie laughed. "Well, he was a simple man and used *password* for all his logins. Besides it's not fair that he should be allowed to go off and have a second family and completely ignore his first son, is it? This way, it's his helicopter account, and it's his emails. And to bankroll this project it was his bank accounts. That's how I hired my guy. Then he hired his crew. Little things I paid for myself but things like the listening devices I ordered online using my ex's credit card."

"Jesus," Keane said from the table.

"You guys figured that out, didn't you?" She laughed. "That's okay. I've had a bit of time to play with this."

"But I guess the last bit to figure out," Nico said, "is what about Charlotte's original assistant?"

"Oh, her. God, she was such an idiot. She messed up your accounts. Do you know how much work it was to fix everything that she did wrong?" she asked Charlotte. "Have no assistant if what you'll hire is that bad."

Charlotte pinched the bridge of her nose. "Please tell me that you didn't kill her."

"Well, I didn't kill her. I hit her with my car, but I didn't kill her. She was still alive, but I walked away."

"But she died from her injuries," Nico said, "so you did kill her."

"No," Maggie said, completely distancing herself from the truth. "That's not how this works. You see? I hit her, and I got out and checked on her. She was pleading for help, and I told her that I would get some, and I walked away. She was still alive. She died with a smile on her face, and I imagine because she thought help was coming that she would be okay."

Charlotte realized there was just no talking logic to this woman. Maggie had absolutely no interest in seeing the results of her actions for what they really were, which in this case was murder. "So then you met me at the coffee shop all those times and offered your services, and, once you were my assistant, you arranged for Australia."

"Absolutely," she said. "I was really pleased to make it all finally happen in six months' time of working with you too."

"True," Charlotte said. "It had been a long time before something else came along that would send me to Australia."

"Exactly," she said. "So, in this way, it's not a bad deal. Now I just have to finish off the job."

"But we're not in Australia," Charlotte said.

That stumped Maggie for a moment. And then she nodded and said, "No, we aren't, but that's okay. I figure I could find another way to dispose of your body that will have just as much impact."

"I hate to even ask," Charlotte said faintly.

"Then don't," she said. "Just die."

And the woman lifted the handgun and fired.

NICO HAD SEEN Maggie raise her arm, and, having heard her words, he'd been primed. As soon as that arm went up, he pushed Charlotte to the floor, following her down and rolling her under the table. He already knew the other two men would jump Maggie. He could hear her crying out, "No, no, she has to die!"

"No." Joshua's voice was hard. "She doesn't. I just found her. I don't want to lose her already."

And Keane said, "The only person here who should die is you. You're one crazy-ass bitch."

Maggie laughed, but it was a maniacal sound that made everybody wince.

Knowing that it was finally safe, Nico crawled out from under the table and helped Charlotte to her feet. He held her in his arms, and they both stared at the woman in front of them. "I'm so sorry for the loss of your son," Charlotte said with tears in her eyes and her voice choking. "But I didn't kill him."

"No, but your actions killed him," she said, completely ignoring the logic of her own actions. "You have to die for what you did."

The two men marched Maggie to the kitchen chair and sat her down, but they didn't let her go.

Joshua looked at Charlotte and asked, "Zip ties?" She walked over to a drawer, then pulled out several. They zipped Maggie to the chair, her legs and hands behind her.

Then Charlotte collapsed beside the woman and said,

"I'm so sorry."

Nico said, "Enough of that. Stop the guilt. This isn't your fault."

"It was something that I couldn't stop either, but this poor woman's life has been ruined."

"I think it was ruined a long time ago," he said gently. "Not everybody survives the loss of a child in the first place."

Charlotte stared, and then comprehension hit her, and she nodded. "I guess that's when it started, isn't it?"

"It definitely is," he said. "So be sympathetic and empathetic but don't feel guilty. That won't help anybody at this point."

She sighed, stood, walked over, and wrapped her arms around him. "How did you get to be so wise?"

"Life," he said. "Sometimes you just have to learn the lessons the hard way. And, in this case, she'll have to learn whatever her lessons are. Those she has yet to learn, I'm sure she'll learn them in her jail cell."

"And me?"

"Well, I'm hoping to set you free," he said with a chuckle. "At least from the guilt. You're not responsible for your husband's death. You're not responsible for how he suffered. You're not responsible for how you suffered or for your response to his suffering. Even before all that, you were not responsible for your parents' deaths or for Joshua being taken away from you. This is all about you letting go of all that guilt and finding out why you do what you do and finding out what you want to do with your life. Not what you feel compelled to do for reasons that are no longer valid."

"Sounds good to me," she said. "Are you planning on being anywhere around at the same time?"

"Well, I was thinking we were going back to that same

conversation about one day, one week, one month at a time?"

"I believe you added one year and a lifetime in there," she said in a teasing voice.

He grinned and wrapped his arms around her, then held her close and whispered, "I'm good with that."

"Me too," she whispered. Then she lifted her head and kissed him gently.

Behind him, he heard Joshua and Keane cheering. Unfortunately Maggie was now crying. He looked over at her and said, "I'm so sorry for what you suffered. But what you've done about it is unforgivable."

And he ushered Charlotte to the living room, where they didn't even have to deal with Maggie. It was time for them to face forward and deal with the good things in life, which, as far as he was concerned, was what they each had together.

EPILOGUE

A WEEK LATER Keane walked down Fisherman's Wharf in Seattle. The place was jam-packed with people, and he wondered what the hell he was doing here. Surely there was a better place for a meeting. Of course, if you want to get lost in a crowd, this was the place to be though. It was overcast with a threat of rain. Still he couldn't, for the life of him, imagine why he was here. But somebody with greater wisdom had decided this, and so a meet up was needed. He walked down the pier where he was expected, and, as he found the spot, he sat down and turned his back on the crowd behind him.

Charlotte and Nico had holed up in Charlotte's house for the last few days, and Keane had been more than happy to take a break. He was eager to join the Mavericks with his own mission to head up and had listened to stories about many other ops from the others who had gone before him. He was okay with that. He was just waiting for it to happen.

When a hand landed on his shoulder, he turned in surprise and looked up to see Lennox staring at him. Keane's eyebrows shot up. "Man, am I glad to see you."

"Good," Lennox said. "Are you willing to work with me too?" He held up an envelope. "We've got orders."

Keane and Lennox sat on the side of the wharf, while the noise of the crowd around them completely faded away.

Keane said, "I was given very little information on it."

"That's because very little is to be had," Lennox admitted. "I've never been on a mission with less information."

"So, what do we know?"

"A group of people went out for a day of sailing. Two of them were washed overboard."

"And the coast guard didn't find them?" Keane asked, staring at Lennox in surprise. "Not terribly unusual, I suppose, given the size of the search area."

Lennox replied, "The coast guard and private yachts haven't seen any sign of them."

"The currents, depending on where they were at the time, could have taken the bodies to any number of places."

"Well, they went missing in Puget Sound," Lennox said.

"Seriously? Puget Sound is interconnected to multiple waterways and basins, not to mention the Pacific Ocean. The currents can change and can run really deep," Keane said. "A search like that involves any number of issues. They may never be found."

"Exactly," Lennox said. "In this case a special request has been made for us to look for them."

Keane gazed at the long lampposts that dotted the pier. "Are you serious?"

Lennox gave him half a grin. "Never more so."

"What? We're in the business of looking for bodies now?" he asked incredulously. "I was expecting to go up against a serial killer or work in the midst of a civil war in a dictator-ruled country or God-only-knows-what, but you're saying my mission is to look for two bodies?" Turning, Keane stared at the water. "Not only that, it's almost impossible to succeed at a job like this."

"Only a couple reasons explain why we're doing this,"

Lennox said, lowering his voice.

"Of course," Keane said. "It's got to be the daughter or niece or nephew to somebody pretty high up the line."

"An admiral," Lennox said. "His daughter and her friend."

"Has he been looking personally?"

"No. He's out on the Baltic Sea, but he's been calling in every favor he could."

"And so a special black-ops mission team of two is to go out into Puget Sound, and possibly beyond into the Pacific Ocean, and look for them?"

"Yes," Lennox replied.

Just then Keane's phone buzzed in his pocket, and he pulled it out to see Nico was calling. Keane lifted the phone to his ear. "Hope you have a better explanation as to why I'm supposed to look for two bodies," Keane snapped.

"So Lennox already told you about the admiral's daughter?"

"Absolutely, but what does this have to do with us? What's wrong with search and rescue, the coast guard or a private recovery company?"

"Because," he said, "they went missing from the same area where two other people went missing just one week ago. Both pairs somewhere in the same area. Plus, we received a distress call from one of those first two who went missing, saying they'd been captured."

Keane slowly straightened. "Captured?"

"Yes," Nico said briskly. "Bodies showed up a few days later, both shot. So we don't know exactly what the hell we've got going on here."

This concludes Book 8 of The Mavericks: Nico.

Read about Keane: The Mavericks, Book 9

The Mavericks: Keane (Book #9)

What happens when the very men—trained to make the hard decisions—come up against the rules and regulations that hold them back from doing what needs to be done? They either stay and work within the constraints given to them or they walk away. Only now, for a select few, they have another option:

The Mavericks. A covert black ops team that steps up and break all the rules … but gets the job done.

Welcome to a new military romance series by *USA Today* best-selling author Dale Mayer. A series where you meet new friends and just might get to meet old ones too in this raw and compelling look at the men who keep us safe every day from the darkness where they operate—and live—in the shadows … until someone special helps them step into the light.

Heading out on a last-ditch rescue mission to Puget Sound one day after two women go overboard in a sailing accident isn't exactly what he'd expected …

But Keane is nothing if not adaptable. He can only hope the two women are alive and doing everything they can to stay that way. Hearing from the local coast guard that more may be involved than just a rescue mission, he and his partner load up and head out to search the waters around the smaller islands off the coast. They have the GPS of the missing women's last-known location, but storms could have sent them anywhere …

Lost, alone—except for her best friend, who's unconscious with a head wound—Sandrine wakes up in a small shelter to find they are locked in. When the door is finally opened, an armed stranger dressed in fatigues dumps a small amount of food and says they are on their own.

Finding the women was one thing, keeping them safe something else again. More is going on in this small island that any of them were expecting … or had planned for …

Find book 9 here!
To find out more visit Dale Mayer's website.
https://geni.us/DMKeaneUniversal

Author's Note

Thank you for reading Nico: The Mavericks, Book 8! If you enjoyed the book, please take a moment and leave a short review.

Dear reader,

I love to hear from readers, and you can contact me at my website: www.dalemayer.com or at my Facebook author page. To be informed of new releases and special offers, sign up for my newsletter or follow me on BookBub. And if you are interested in joining Dale Mayer's Reader Group, here is the Facebook sign up page.
http://geni.us/DaleMayerFBGroup

Cheers,
Dale Mayer

About the Author

Dale Mayer is a *USA Today* best-selling author, best known for her SEALs military romances, her Psychic Visions series, and her Lovely Lethal Garden cozy series. Her contemporary romances are raw and full of passion and emotion (Broken But … Mending, Hathaway House series). Her thrillers will keep you guessing (Kate Morgan, By Death series), and her romantic comedies will keep you giggling (*It's a Dog's Life*, a stand-alone novella; and the Broken Protocols series, starring Charming Marvin, the cat).

Dale honors the stories that come to her—and some of them are crazy, break all the rules and cross multiple genres!

To go with her fiction, she also writes nonfiction in many different fields, with books available on résumé writing, companion gardening, and the US mortgage system. All her books are available in print and ebook format.

Connect with Dale Mayer Online

Dale's Website – www.dalemayer.com
Twitter – @DaleMayer
Facebook Page – geni.us/DaleMayerFBFanPage
Facebook Group – geni.us/DaleMayerFBGroup
BookBub – geni.us/DaleMayerBookbub
Instagram – geni.us/DaleMayerInstagram
Goodreads – geni.us/DaleMayerGoodreads
Newsletter – geni.us/DaleNews

Also by Dale Mayer

Published Adult Books:

Hathaway House

Aaron, Book 1

Brock, Book 2

Cole, Book 3

Denton, Book 4

Elliot, Book 5

Finn, Book 6

Gregory, Book 7

The K9 Files

Ethan, Book 1

Pierce, Book 2

Zane, Book 3

Blaze, Book 4

Lucas, Book 5

Parker, Book 6

Carter, Book 7

Lovely Lethal Gardens

Arsenic in the Azaleas, Book 1

Bones in the Begonias, Book 2

Corpse in the Carnations, Book 3

Daggers in the Dahlias, Book 4

Evidence in the Echinacea, Book 5

Footprints in the Ferns, Book 6

Gun in the Gardenias, Book 7
Handcuffs in the Heather, Book 8

Psychic Vision Series
Tuesday's Child
Hide 'n Go Seek
Maddy's Floor
Garden of Sorrow
Knock Knock…
Rare Find
Eyes to the Soul
Now You See Her
Shattered
Into the Abyss
Seeds of Malice
Eye of the Falcon
Itsy-Bitsy Spider
Unmasked
Deep Beneath
From the Ashes
Psychic Visions Books 1–3
Psychic Visions Books 4–6
Psychic Visions Books 7–9

By Death Series
Touched by Death
Haunted by Death
Chilled by Death
By Death Books 1–3

Broken Protocols – Romantic Comedy Series
Cat's Meow
Cat's Pajamas

Cat's Cradle

Cat's Claus

Broken Protocols 1-4

Broken and… Mending

Skin

Scars

Scales (of Justice)

Broken but… Mending 1-3

Glory

Genesis

Tori

Celeste

Glory Trilogy

Biker Blues

Morgan: Biker Blues, Volume 1

Cash: Biker Blues, Volume 2

SEALs of Honor

Mason: SEALs of Honor, Book 1

Hawk: SEALs of Honor, Book 2

Dane: SEALs of Honor, Book 3

Swede: SEALs of Honor, Book 4

Shadow: SEALs of Honor, Book 5

Cooper: SEALs of Honor, Book 6

Markus: SEALs of Honor, Book 7

Evan: SEALs of Honor, Book 8

Mason's Wish: SEALs of Honor, Book 9

Chase: SEALs of Honor, Book 10

Brett: SEALs of Honor, Book 11

Devlin: SEALs of Honor, Book 12

Easton: SEALs of Honor, Book 13
Ryder: SEALs of Honor, Book 14
Macklin: SEALs of Honor, Book 15
Corey: SEALs of Honor, Book 16
Warrick: SEALs of Honor, Book 17
Tanner: SEALs of Honor, Book 18
Jackson: SEALs of Honor, Book 19
Kanen: SEALs of Honor, Book 20
Nelson: SEALs of Honor, Book 21
Taylor: SEALs of Honor, Book 22
SEALs of Honor, Books 1–3
SEALs of Honor, Books 4–6
SEALs of Honor, Books 7–10
SEALs of Honor, Books 11–13
SEALs of Honor, Books 14–16
SEALs of Honor, Books 17–19

Heroes for Hire

Levi's Legend: Heroes for Hire, Book 1
Stone's Surrender: Heroes for Hire, Book 2
Merk's Mistake: Heroes for Hire, Book 3
Rhodes's Reward: Heroes for Hire, Book 4
Flynn's Firecracker: Heroes for Hire, Book 5
Logan's Light: Heroes for Hire, Book 6
Harrison's Heart: Heroes for Hire, Book 7
Saul's Sweetheart: Heroes for Hire, Book 8
Dakota's Delight: Heroes for Hire, Book 9
Michael's Mercy (Part of Sleeper SEAL Series)
Tyson's Treasure: Heroes for Hire, Book 10
Jace's Jewel: Heroes for Hire, Book 11
Rory's Rose: Heroes for Hire, Book 12
Brandon's Bliss: Heroes for Hire, Book 13

Liam's Lily: Heroes for Hire, Book 14

North's Nikki: Heroes for Hire, Book 15

Anders's Angel: Heroes for Hire, Book 16

Reyes's Raina: Heroes for Hire, Book 17

Dezi's Diamond: Heroes for Hire, Book 18

Vince's Vixen: Heroes for Hire, Book 19

Ice's Icing: Heroes for Hire, Book 20

Heroes for Hire, Books 1–3

Heroes for Hire, Books 4–6

Heroes for Hire, Books 7–9

Heroes for Hire, Books 10–12

Heroes for Hire, Books 13–15

SEALs of Steel

Badger: SEALs of Steel, Book 1

Erick: SEALs of Steel, Book 2

Cade: SEALs of Steel, Book 3

Talon: SEALs of Steel, Book 4

Laszlo: SEALs of Steel, Book 5

Geir: SEALs of Steel, Book 6

Jager: SEALs of Steel, Book 7

The Final Reveal: SEALs of Steel, Book 8

SEALs of Steel, Books 1–4

SEALs of Steel, Books 5–8

SEALs of Steel, Books 1–8

The Mavericks

Kerrick, Book 1

Griffin, Book 2

Jax, Book 3

Beau, Book 4

Asher, Book 5

Ryker, Book 6

Miles, Book 7
Nico, Book 8
Keane, Book 9
Lennox, Book 10
Gavin, Book 11
Shane, Book 12

Collections
Dare to Be You…
Dare to Love…
Dare to be Strong…
RomanceX3

Standalone Novellas
It's a Dog's Life
Riana's Revenge
Second Chances

Published Young Adult Books:

Family Blood Ties Series
Vampire in Denial
Vampire in Distress
Vampire in Design
Vampire in Deceit
Vampire in Defiance
Vampire in Conflict
Vampire in Chaos
Vampire in Crisis
Vampire in Control
Vampire in Charge
Family Blood Ties Set 1–3
Family Blood Ties Set 1–5

Family Blood Ties Set 4–6

Family Blood Ties Set 7–9

Sian's Solution, A Family Blood Ties Series Prequel
    Novelette

Design series

Dangerous Designs

Deadly Designs

Darkest Designs

Design Series Trilogy

Standalone

In Cassie's Corner

Gem Stone (a Gemma Stone Mystery)

Time Thieves

Published Non-Fiction Books:

Career Essentials

Career Essentials: The Résumé

Career Essentials: The Cover Letter

Career Essentials: The Interview

Career Essentials: 3 in 1